Bello:
hidden talent rediscovered!

Bello is a digital only imprint of Pan Macmillan,
established to breathe new life into previously published,
classic books.

At Bello we believe in the timeless power of the imagination,
of good story, narrative and entertainment and we want to use
digital technology to ensure that many more readers
can enjoy these books into the future.

We publish in ebook and Print on Demand formats
to bring these wonderful books to new audiences.

About Bello:

www.panmacmillan.com/imprints/bello

About the author:

www.panmacmillan.com/author/francisdurbridge

Francis Durbridge

Francis Henry Durbridge was an English playwright and author born in Hull. In 1938, he created the character Paul Temple for the BBC radio serial *Send for Paul Temple*.

A crime novelist and detective, the gentlemanly Temple solved numerous crimes with the help of Steve Trent, a Fleet Street journalist who later became his wife. The character proved enormously popular and appeared in 16 radio serials and later spawned a 64-part big-budget television series (1969–71) and radio productions, as well as a number of comic strips, four feature films and various foreign radio productions.

Francis Durbridge also had a successful career as a writer for the stage and screen. His most successful play, *Suddenly at Home*, ran in London's West End for over a year.

Francis Durbridge

THE OTHER MAN

BELL

First published in 1957 by Hodder & Stoughton

This edition published 2012 by Bello
an imprint of Pan Macmillan, a division of Macmillan Publishers Limited
Pan Macmillan, 20 New Wharf Road, London N1 9RR
Basingstoke and Oxford
Associated companies throughout the world

www.panmacmillan.com/imprints/bello
www.curtisbrown.co.uk

ISBN 978-1-4472-1623-0 POD

Copyright © Francis Durbridge, 1957

The right of Francis Durbridge to be identified as the
author of this work has been asserted in accordance
with the Copyright, Designs and Patents Act 1988.

Chapter One

On the outskirts of Medlow and in some of the loveliest country in Buckinghamshire stands Rockingham College. Although not as well known to the general public as certain other English public schools, Rockingham's record is a proud one; for a century and a half it has fed young men of integrity and intelligence into a wide variety of honourable professions. The subaltern leading his patrol in Malaya, the overworked and underpaid curate in East London and the District Officer in one of the remoter parts of Africa may well have been educated at Rockingham. Three Lieutenant-Generals, an Air Chief Marshal, a Newspaper Editor, the Managing Director of an International Airline, and two Cabinet Ministers were prepared for their onerous responsibilities there. Two large memorials testify to the fighting qualities of Old Rockinghamians.

David Henderson, D.S.C., B.A. (Oxon.), emerged from one of the classrooms after the last work period of the day. He paused for a moment in the quadrangle and looked about him with satisfaction: everything about Rockingham was secure and everlasting even in this troubled year. He even thought of that intellectual desert, the Lower Fifth, with something like affection. The Lower Fifth consisted of boys aged fifteen and a half and sixteen and it was part of Henderson's duty to urge them towards the Sixth form. In many cases it was an uphill and unrewarding task but Henderson would not have had it otherwise. Under his arm were Lower Fifth's exercise books which promised some interesting reading for him that evening. The subject Henderson had set was "How I would go about making England a better country to live in"; there should, he thought cynically, be some *real* gems among this lot. . . .

David Henderson was thirty-eight, a shade under six feet tall and deceptively slim. His hair, which was black, was beginning to recede slightly; his eyes a particularly dark blue.

When David Henderson came down from Oxford with a casually acquired Honours Degree in English Literature, an illustrious academic career was forecast for him. But 1940 found him unacademically engaged in the Battle of the Atlantic in corvettes. After three years' almost continuous sea service he found himself attached to one of the less orthodox sections of the Navy.

Since his demobilization Henderson's horizon had been bounded by boys to the exclusion of everything else. His undoubted flair for handling these incalculable creatures combined with an ability to impart knowledge interestingly to even the most slothful backslider of Lower Fifth had soon secured for him the post of Housemaster at Rockingham. In this capacity he had proved an unqualified success; so much so, in fact, that many parents entering their sons for Rockingham asked tentatively if there were vacancies in "Henderson's".

Henderson never deliberately sought popularity. But he earnestly believed, unlike some public schoolmasters, that intimidation and sarcasm played no part in the moulding of a boy's character. The cane he used sparingly and reluctantly but on very rare occasions with devastating and lasting effect.

As Henderson neared the entrance to his house he grinned gently to himself. The boy waiting in his study was in all probability expecting a caning within the next few minutes.

Roger Ford was waiting at the entrance of the study as Henderson came round the corner. His expression suggested that the outcome of the forthcoming interview with his housemaster was a foregone conclusion. "It is a far, far better thing that I do. . . ." Sydney Carton to the life, thought David Henderson indulgently.

Roger Ford was the son of a detective-inspector of some repute and owed his presence at Rockingham College almost entirely to Henderson. A detective-inspector's salary rarely permits a public school education for his son, but as a result of Henderson's coaching young Ford had achieved a scholarship. In common with almost every schoolmaster Henderson had his favourites amongst his boys, but was at pains to conceal the fact from them. Roger Ford was by way of being one of his favourites.

He was a tall, grave-faced boy with an intelligent face and an oddly disarming manner. He shuffled his feet and moistened his lips at Henderson's approach.

"Ah, Ford," said Henderson. "Come on in, will you?"

The boy murmured "Yes, sir," and followed the master into the study.

Henderson had experienced his fair share of hard living and liked comfort when he could get it. His study was spacious, not aggressively bachelor in appearance, and radiated comfort. Roger Ford thought it would be nice to sit down to some tea and toast. As things were, sitting down might present certain difficulties in the near future.

"It's a pity to get into trouble right at the end of the term," observed Henderson. He hung up his gown and sat himself at his desk. He regarded the boy with a calmly judicial look. Your number's up, Roger, thought the boy. He's just going to do a bit of the cat and mouse stuff first and then—six of the best.

Ah well, it didn't last long. . . .

"I'm sorry, sir," said Ford at length.

"Mr. Granger recommends that I beat you," continued his tormentor. "Not at all sure that I shouldn't, as a matter of fact."

"No, sir," said Ford. "I mean yes, sir."

"After all," continued Henderson, "if every boy pushed another boy into the swimming pool just because he didn't like him where would our discipline be?"

Roger Ford searched his mind for a reply that seemed neither fearful nor flippant and eventually settled for: "Where indeed, sir?"

Henderson's sudden smile flashed across his face. He said: "Since it's the end of term and Justin Major probably asked for it we'll overlook the matter."

Ford relaxed visibly.

"But next time you see Justin Major bending over the swimming pool control your natural impulses, Ford. Understand?"

"Yes, sir."

"Good. Now then, what about some tea and toast?"

"Thanks awfully, sir."

A jolly good chap, old Henderson. One of the best.

The tea and toast were produced with seemingly miraculous speed by Mrs. Williams, Henderson's housekeeper, and with them she brought a small package.

"For you, sir," she said. "Just come by registered post."

Henderson studied the package for a moment and then placed it on his desk. "Thanks, Mrs. Williams."

"If you don't want me for anything more," said Mrs. Williams, "I think I'll just nip into Medlow."

Henderson nodded. "That's perfectly all right." He smiled at Ford who was staring at the buttered toast. "You can start, Ford."

After a little while Henderson finished his tea and lit his pipe. "Anyone coming to fetch you Thursday morning, Ford?"

"Yes, sir. My father."

"Good. What time?"

"Seven o'clock, sir."

"Seven o'clock? That's rather early even for a detective-inspector, isn't it?"

"Oh, my father's a very early riser, sir," said Roger, idly opening a book on the table beside him and glancing at the fly-leaf.

"If you'd like to borrow that book," said Henderson. "Just say so."

Roger looked up with a guilty start. "Well, as a matter of fact I would rather like to, sir. It looks jolly interesting."

"It is," said Henderson. "Help yourself."

The boy picked up the book and looked at the fly-leaf again. "Could you tell me what this is, sir?"

"A dirty mark occasioned by the impact of a recently buttered finger!"

Ford grinned sheepishly. "Sorry, sir," he said. "I actually meant what does this quotation mean?"

"Quotation?" said Henderson, "what quotation?"

"This, sir. '*Suavitor in modo, fortiter in re ...*'"

4

"Let me see," said Henderson quietly. He looked in the fly-leaf of the book and for a moment his eyes narrowed. Then he smiled at Roger.

"It means 'gentle in the manner, but vigorous in the deed.' " He looked at the writing again. " 'Gentle in the manner but vigorous in the deed,' " he said quietly. "I'm not sure that isn't an improvement on the school motto."

Henderson passed the book back to Roger and glanced at his watch.

"You'd better cut off, young Ford," he said. "I've got twenty-five vilely written and misspelt essays to wade through and it's time I started on them."

When Roger Ford had left the room Henderson glanced idly at the first essay in the pile. He smiled as he read the first sentence; evidently Sinclair Minor, the somewhat truculent son of a Socialist Member of Parliament, proposed certain sweeping changes in the country's future education scheme. Then suddenly and abruptly he slapped his hand down on the pile of essays and almost regretfully turned to the small package that had arrived by the afternoon post.

The wrapping revealed a man's wristlet watch. Henderson studied it for a moment or two then unfastened his own wristlet watch and strapped the new one on to his wrist. From a drawer in the desk he took out a small leather notebook and an automatic—a .32 of Spanish make. His manner was calm, deliberate, unhurried. He shot another quick glance at the pile of essays and expelled a barely audible sigh; almost it seemed that he deplored the contemplation of a lethal weapon and would prefer to be reading, marking, and inwardly digesting Sinclair Minor's plans for reform. Finally he put his own watch in a drawer and examined the automatic. He was examining it with the sure touch of one who is no stranger to firearms when the telephone rang.

Henderson picked up the receiver. He said: "Hallo. . .? Henderson speaking."

A precise and cultured voice said: "This is Cooper."

Henderson said: "Ah. . . ." There was an air of finality about his voice as if he were finally relegating Lower Fifth's essays to the back of his mind.

"Have you got the watch?" said the voice at the other end.

Henderson fingered the watch for a moment. "Yes, it's just arrived. Are we in time, d'you think?"

Cooper's voice became crisp and incisive. "We'll have to take a chance. Can you go there at once?"

"Yes," said Henderson.

"Right. I'll see you there."

Cooper hung up with a decisive click. Henderson glanced at the watch on his wrist and picked up the automatic.

The houseboats on the river at Medlow have an idle and carefree elegance that is all their own. Nothing disturbs their serene anchorage. At week-ends tired City businessmen find that they are not so tired as they thought they were—the tiredness manifests itself on Monday morning; the young and not so young frolic discreetly; illicit friendships flourish. There is always love and laughter in plenty on the river at Medlow and the few permanent houseboat residents regard the junketing with aloof tolerance. It is almost impossible to imagine anything sinister happening in this little flesh-pot of the Thames which one of the more enterprising of the houseboat-agents describes as "a natural paradise".

Katherine Walters would have agreed with this house-agent's assessment on this particular afternoon. She was reclining in a punt which she had manoeuvred into the shade of a large tree. Only one houseboat was in her immediate vision and she had noticed its name as she had drifted down river: *High Tor*. It was painted white and looked cool and inviting. Idly Katherine wondered who lived in it.

She was reading a novel that was agreeably beguiling but not so absorbing as to intrude on the magic of the afternoon. Every so often she dipped a well-manicured hand into the water. Apart from an occasional rowing boat idling backwards and forwards the river seemed completely deserted.

Katherine Walters was an attractive woman in the late twenties.

Her complexion and figure bordered on perfection but her cheek bones were a fraction too high and stopped her from being conventionally good looking. She had a good mouth, full and generous, but her dark brown eyes wore a slightly tired look.

David Henderson stood in the middle of the living-room of the houseboat called *High Tor*. The normally well furnished room was in a state of indescribable confusion. The writing desk had evidently been ransacked with wanton thoroughness; chairs had been overturned; a carpet had been ripped from the floor. A handsome cocktail cabinet had been upended and a standard lamp lolled drunkenly over the back of a sofa.

Henderson looked thoughtfully at the body of a man lying in the middle of the floor. The only description possible was that of an apparently youngish man of medium height, for little of his original features remained. He had obviously been battered about the face and head with a blunt instrument.

Henderson knelt by the body. He removed the wristlet watch he had been wearing and strapped it to the wrist of the dead man. He then rose, cast a final, critical, and all-embracing look round the room and went out on to the deck of the houseboat.

Katherine Walters closed her book and yawned. On a cooler afternoon she might have been able to give her undivided attention to the unco-ordinated antics of an unstable young woman who was in love with three men at the same time, but the heat had induced in her a pleasant feeling of drowsiness.

She glanced towards the houseboat called *High Tor* and saw the figure of a man who had just come up on deck. She studied him idly for a moment. She saw that he was tall, dark and quite good looking. The soporific atmosphere of the river precluded any real interest in tall, dark and good looking men on houseboats but Katherine continued to watch him disinterestedly.

The man glanced quickly in her direction and then fell to watching the bank of the river. His attitude was casual and relaxed. Probably waiting for a girl friend, diagnosed Katherine with somnolent romanticism.

Presently a car appeared on the road which ran parallel to the river. The man on the houseboat took a last look in Katherine's direction and then turned and raised a hand in greeting to the driver. Finally he went ashore and climbed into the car. Katherine yawned, picked up her book again and forgot about the entire episode. . . .

The police quickly arrived at *High Tor* and with their usual patience and thoroughness started to take measurements and photographs of the living-room. The police surgeon had already been and given the usual banal and non-committal verdict: the man had died from repeated blows, presumably from a blunt instrument, about the head and face. The exact time of death was impossible to judge and an autopsy would be necessary. It was the usual story with very few variations and the police surgeon had long since lost count of how many similar murders he had been called in on. He was merely summoned for the purpose of pronouncing life extinct and to hazard a guess as to when death had taken place. This particular corpse, with its head and face practically battered to pulp, had called for little specialized medical knowledge. One of these days, thought the police surgeon with weary cynicism, they'll fetch me to look at a body that isn't *quite* dead. But that rarely if ever happened; they were either shot or knifed or poisoned or had their brains bashed out. The body in *High Tor* represented as thorough a job of killing as the police surgeon had ever seen. He did not linger long on the houseboat because he was required at the police station to give his considered opinion as to whether a motorist had been drunk or sober when he had collided with a "Keep Left" sign. Dead or drunk, it was just another job.

Detective-Inspector Michael Ford was examining the contents of a small writing bureau in the corner of the living-room. His movements were unhurried and deceptively casual. Twenty-five years in the police force, fifteen of which had been spent in the C.I.D., had taught him that things are very seldom what they seem and in murder cases practically never. He had learned that the solution of such cases often depended on cigarette ends, trouser buttons, broken mirrors and old pieces of blotting paper. With a little sigh, in which there was more than a suspicion of cynicism, he foresaw the wearisome days, weeks, months and even years of patient and painstaking inquiries which would inevitably follow the discovery of this body which had met with such savage violence. Clues would be found, followed up and discarded as worthless. The superintendent would get liverish and the Popular Press would harangue the police for taking so long to make an arrest. A seemingly endless procession of people would be interviewed, produce alibis, tell lies and be finally cleared of suspicion. On the face of it this one looked like being one of the more tedious cases attended by the usual lack of sleep and irregular meals that went with all murder cases.

Ford was forty-fivish, dark, heavily built and dependable looking. His expression was habitually stern but he periodically produced a smile of rare charm. His manner was quiet and uncompromising. He had a hard-won reputation for never giving up hope of solving a case. On several occasions seemingly insoluble crimes—crimes without apparent motives or suspects—had been handed over to Ford with entirely satisfactory results.

The detective-constable who had been taking photographs packed up his equipment. Ford looked up from the writing bureau.

"All finished, Morris?"

"Yes, sir."

"If you see Sergeant Broderick outside ask him to come in for a moment."

Detective-Sergeant Broderick strode jauntily into the living-room. He was a tall, sharp-featured man with an incisive and energetic manner. He radiated confidence and self-assurance. Broderick had risen to his present rank at the surprisingly early age of twenty-nine and Ford thought a little ruefully of the ten years he had spent on the beat becoming even a detective-constable. Broderick's forceful personality and intelligence would undoubtedly take him far in his profession, thought Ford. A little too impatient at times, possibly slightly too sure of himself, but a first-rate detective for all that. Ford was always glad to have Broderick working with him on any case.

"Ah, there you are," said Ford looking up from the writing bureau. "A messy sort of job."

"Messy is right," said Broderick. "Doctor been?"

"Yes, they sent Jennings."

"Well, I suppose he knows a stiff when he sees one." Apparently Broderick had a poor opinion of the police surgeon. "What did he say?"

"Usual story. Impossible to say without an autopsy and even then it might be difficult."

"He's improving," said Broderick generously. He jerked his head towards the body. "I suppose he really *is* dead?"

"You'll never see a deader one," said Ford drily. "Now, what have you found out so far?"

Broderick produced a notebook with a flourish.

"The dead man's an Italian, name of Rocello," he said. "He's been in these parts for nearly a fortnight. This boat belongs to someone called James Cooper."

Ford nodded. "I know Cooper. Seen him in the village. Short, rather distinguished-looking bird with a long nose."

"That's him," said Broderick. He consulted his notebook again. "It seems he's a solicitor and works for a firm called Dawson, Wyman and Clewes."

"Hmm . . . local firm?"

"No, London—Sloane Square. Pretty smart sort of practice I should think."

"Oh? What makes you think that?"

Broderick waved a hand round the living-room. "Well, look at this lot. Must take a bit of money to keep a little nest like this."

"I suppose it does. Now, what about this Rocello character. Was he a friend of Cooper's?"

"Seems like it. According to Mrs. Prothero—she's the old girl who keeps the shop in the High Street—Cooper went back to London last Wednesday and left Rocello in charge of the houseboat."

Ford frowned. "Last Wednesday, eh? But didn't Cooper come down for the week-end?"

"Apparently not. This Mrs. Prothero has two or three lock-up garages and Cooper usually parks his car in one of them."

"I see." Ford looked at the body again and then at Broderick. "This looks like being a tough one, Bob."

Broderick shrugged. "We've had 'em tougher."

Ford smiled. There was always something infectious about Broderick's confidence. Of course, he'd had it nice and lucky so far in his career as a detective. Broderick had managed to solve two particularly baffling cases recently, both of them with a minimum of leg work and soul-destroying routine inquiry. Sometimes you were fortunate enough to get a case in which everything fell neatly into place but this one didn't seem to come into that comfortable category.

Ford took two pieces of paper from his breast pocket. One was the routine occurrence report from the uniform man who had been first on the scene. The Superintendent, who was not given to verbosity on paper, had written on it "D.I. Ford please inquire". That was the superintendent's way of giving him an absolutely free hand to conduct the investigation as he thought fit. Better than some of these chairborne geniuses who badgered you from morning till night and expected the whole thing, complete with suspect, motive and statements, to be buttoned up within seventy-two hours. The writing on the other piece of paper was in Ford's own hand. It said:

Katherine Walters—see anything?
Doctor Sheldon?
Barker Brothers?
Car. Anyone see driver?
Henderson—Italy.
Cooper?

He noted, wryly, that there seemed to be a lot of question marks. He said to Broderick: "Not much more we can do today, Bob. We'll get started properly tomorrow. . . ."

Chapter Two

A fairly representative bag, thought Doctor Richard Sheldon with a trace of cynicism as he left his surgery after the last patient had departed. Two embryo duodenal ulcers occasioned by worry over income tax, an overweight woman in need of exercise and three children with chicken-pox.

Richard Sheldon was a country General Practitioner of the older school. Grey of hair and comfortable of figure, he had the enviable knack of making his patients feel better as a result of having seen him. The mother of the last chicken-pox-afflicted child had induced in him a desire for a glass of sherry. He was just reaching for the decanter when the front door bell rang. More chicken-pox, diagnosed the doctor pessimistically.

"There's a gentleman from the police to see you, sir," announced the parlour-maid with ill concealed excitement.

Sheldon's glass was half-way to his lips. "A policeman to see me?" he said. "Now, what can I have done wrong?"

The maid giggled. "He's a plain-clothes man, a detective," she elaborated.

"Well, at least that means I haven't left my car where I shouldn't," said Sheldon. "You'd better ask him to come in, Judy." A sudden thought struck him. "Perhaps you'd bring another glass. There must be a policeman somewhere in England who'll accept a glass of sherry when on duty."

Judy appeared with the glass and Inspector Ford. She lingered hopefully for a moment but was dismissed by a nod from Sheldon.

"Doctor Sheldon?" said Ford briskly. "I'm Detective-Inspector Ford. I hope I'm not disturbing you when you're busy."

"Not at all," murmured Sheldon. "Er—have a glass of sherry, won't you?"

"That will be very acceptable, sir," said Ford.

"Excellent," said Sheldon. He busied himself with the decanter. "I've often wondered why policemen never accept a drink when they're making inquiries."

"It's not universal, Doctor Sheldon," said Ford. They toasted one another gravely. "You're probably wondering why I'm here, sir."

"I must confess to being a little curious," admitted Sheldon. "How exactly can I help you?"

"I understand you have a young lady staying with you, sir—a Miss Walters."

"That's right. She's my niece."

"Do you think I could have a word with her?"

"Yes, by all means. But what exactly—?"

"No need to be alarmed, sir," reassured Ford. "I just want to ask her a few questions—purely routine stuff. I'm investigating the murder on the houseboat *High Tor*."

"Ah, yes," said Sheldon. "I was talking to Katherine about it only this morning. The murdered man was an Italian, wasn't he?"

"That's right, sir. His name was Paul Rocello. He was staying with a Mr. Cooper."

"Cooper," said the doctor thoughtfully. "I've met him, I think. Was Rocello a friend of his?"

"So we believe. But our information's rather secondhand at the moment because we haven't been able to contact Cooper."

"I'm afraid I can't help you over that, Inspector," said Sheldon. "I thought he worked for a firm of solicitors but apart from that I know very little about him."

"We *thought* Mr. Cooper worked for a firm of solicitors too," said Ford.

"Oh? And doesn't he?"

Ford changed the subject adroitly and pleasantly. "I think if you don't mind, sir, I'll tell you why I want a word with Miss Walters. I understand she hired a punt yesterday and spent an hour or so on the river."

"Did she?" said the doctor. "I know she went out in the afternoon but I didn't know she went on the river."

With a faint smile, Ford produced a notebook. "She hired a punt from Barker Brothers and was on the river from half-past two until about four o'clock. At least, that's according to our information."

"I'm sure your information is correct, Inspector," said Sheldon. "No doubt you know exactly what I was doing then as well."

"Yes indeed, sir," said Ford. The slight twinkle in his eyes belied the seriousness of his tone. "You were in your surgery until quarter to four and then you came in here for a cup of tea."

"I have a wholesome regard for our police force," murmured Sheldon. "You're perfectly right."

"It wasn't a bad guess, sir," said Ford. They both laughed. Ford went on: "Has Miss Walters been staying with you long, sir?"

"Not very long. Her father—that's my brother—died rather suddenly and unfortunately—" he broke off as Katherine came into the room. "Ah, there you are, my dear. This is Inspector Ford. He wants to ask you a few questions."

Katherine eyed the newcomer in surprise.

"Questions?" she repeated, taken aback.

"It's about the murder on the houseboat, Miss," explained Ford somewhat apologetically, noting her intelligent eyes and sensitive mouth.

"Just a matter of routine, Miss," he added with a smile. "Always the same in a murder case. We have to question hundreds of people, in the hope we might get something to work on."

"Well, I don't think I can be of much help," said Katherine. "But I'll answer anything I can."

"That's fine," said Ford. "I understand you spent part of yesterday afternoon on the river. Is that correct?"

Katherine nodded. "Perfectly," she said. "It was a glorious afternoon so I hired a punt."

"And moored it about fifty yards from *High Tor*."

"*High Tor?*"

"That's the houseboat where the murder was committed."

"What, that lovely white one?"

"That's the one. Now, what I want to know, Miss Walters, is whether you saw or heard anything that aroused your suspicions in any way?"

"Not a thing, I'm afraid. But I did see a man on deck, now I come to think of it."

Ford's bushy black eyebrows slid together to form one line. "You saw a man, did you?"

"Yes," replied Katherine.

"What was he doing?"

"He came up on deck and stood there for a moment. Then he waved to someone in a car on the bridge. He left the houseboat, got into the car and they drove away. That's all I saw."

"It's something to be going on with," commented Ford. "What time was this?"

"About half-past three, I should think."

Doctor Sheldon rubbed his nose thoughtfully. "What time was the murder committed, Inspector?" he asked.

"Hard to say, sir. Probably between one o'clock on Wednesday morning and four o'clock on Thursday afternoon."

"Not very definite, is it?"

"It's the best the police surgeon could do for us, sir."

"I really must apologize for asking questions," said Sheldon, "after all, I'm supposed to be answering them. But could you tell me how this man was killed?"

"That's perfectly all right, sir," said Ford. "It seems that there had been a straggle and he'd been hit across the face, possibly with the butt of a revolver." He turned to Katherine again. "You didn't recognize this man, I suppose."

"No, I'd never seen him before."

"Can you describe him?"

"I only just caught a glimpse of his face when he turned round in my direction." Katherine looked apologetically at Ford. "I really am trying my best to be helpful but I wasn't to know that there was a dead body fifty yards away from me."

"I quite understand, Miss Walters," said Ford. "And you're being very helpful indeed." There was no place, he thought a shade bitterly, for beautiful young women in murder investigations. A girl like this, for instance, should be free to laze around in a punt, go to dances with boy friends and live a pleasant, sheltered existence away from weary police investigators asking silly questions. Ford sighed mentally. The only thing he had to do was bring the murderer to justice and he'd have to ask a lot more damn' fool questions before this particular killer was in the dock.

"I won't bother you for much longer, Miss Walters," said Ford. "Now, this car that was waiting. Did you see the driver?"

"I'm afraid not. You see, it was very hot, and I was reading a book most of the time. I wasn't really taking much interest in anything."

Ford smiled suddenly. "I have occasional afternoons like that myself, Miss Walters. In fact, I was due for a holiday when this murder cropped up. Did you see what sort of car it was?"

Katherine said: "Yes, it was a saloon. I definitely noticed that."

"Colour?"

"Dark. Either black or dark blue." She looked appealingly at Ford. "I know what you're thinking. About every other car on the road is a dark saloon. I only *wish* I could be more helpful."

"You're doing very well, Miss Walters." The deep-set eyes under their thick, black eye-lashes looked straight into her own. "One thing more. Would you recognize the man you saw on the houseboat again if you saw him?"

Katherine answered after a barely perceptible pause.

"Yes, I think I would, Inspector. . . ."

Chapter Three

David Henderson sat at his desk correcting the history essays of the Lower Fifth. Occasionally he chuckled at some outrageous pronouncement about the habits of the Hanovers, periodically he sighed over some howler of grammar or punctuation. From time to time he made antiseptic marginal notes with a blue pencil. On the whole, however, he found the history essays more entertaining than his new library book. He had decided on the subject for the next essay: "America's Influence as a World Power". That should be *really* entertaining.

"It was a funny thing, but the King of France at that time could only just talk French...." Mortimer Campbell had penned in a spidery hand. Funny indeed, thought Henderson. He was just sharpening his blue pencil for another onslaught when Mrs. Williams poked her head round the door. "Mr. Ford's here and would like to see you, sir," she announced.

Henderson looked up. "Mr. Ford?"

"Yes, sir. Could you spare him a few minutes?"

"Of course. Ask him to come in, will you?"

Ford smiled cheerfully at Henderson as they shook hands. "I hope I'm not disturbing you when you're busy," said the inspector.

"Not at all," said Henderson. "When I'm correcting history essays a respite is very welcome."

Ford grinned. "I can believe that, sir," he said. "Got to Roger's yet?"

"That," said Henderson, "is a pleasure in store for me. Oh, and before I forget—Roger's expecting you on Thursday morning. Seven o'clock."

"I'll be there. How's the boy getting on?"

"First rate. A bit shaky on Latin, though."

"Can't see that Latin matters much," observed Ford. "All I know is *Habeas Corpus* and that's served me all right since I've been a policeman."

"Frankly, I agree with you," said Henderson. "But not a word to Roger. Incidentally, was it about Roger you came to see me?"

"Well, no, sir, it wasn't. I expect you've heard about the murder on the houseboat."

Henderson said: "Yes, indeed I have. So they've put you in charge of that, have they?"

"That's right, sir."

"And you think I can help you solve it? Detection's not much in my line, I'm afraid."

"It's mostly a matter of common sense," said Ford modestly. "Now, sir. The murdered man was an Italian, name of Paul Rocello. He came from Venice. I seem to remember you telling me that you'd spent some time in Italy—Venice, I believe you said, sir."

"Yes, I was in Italy from April '44 until December '46," said Henderson. He sounded mildly surprised. "Why d'you ask?"

"I just wondered if you'd heard of the name Rocello whilst you were in Venice?"

Henderson looked amused. "Venice is a very large place, Inspector."

"I suppose it is, sir. I just thought it might be a common name in those parts."

"It very probably is," said Henderson. "I'm afraid I'm not being terribly helpful, Inspector. Try me with something else."

Ford smiled. "This might be more your line of country." He produced a piece of paper from his pocket. "This inscription was written on the back of the dead man's wristlet watch. All I know is that it's in Latin. But the standard of Latin in the police force is—er—not of the highest. So perhaps you'd translate it for us."

Henderson took the piece of paper and looked at it. "Let's see, now," he said. " '*Suavitor in modo, fortiter in re.*' Damned if my own Latin isn't a bit rusty—my principal function is to instil the rudiments of English into these vandals, you know. But I think I can manage this one for you. It means 'gentle in the manner, but vigorous in the deed'."

" 'Gentle in the manner, but vigorous in the deed,' eh?" said Ford grimly. "Very appropriate, in the circumstances. The murderer was certainly vigorous in the deed, all right. He smashed the poor devil's face in." He took the piece of paper from Henderson. "Many thanks, Mr. Henderson. Sorry to have troubled you."

"Any time, Inspector," said Henderson. "An intriguing case, I should think."

"That's putting it mildly, sir," said Ford. He picked up his hat. "At the moment the nigger in the woodpile seems to be Cooper, the owner of the houseboat. A real mystery man. Everyone in these parts thought he was a solicitor and worked for a firm called Dawson, Wyman and Clewes."

"And doesn't he?"

"They've never heard of him."

"So that makes him Suspect Number One, does it?"

"I wouldn't go so far as to say that, sir," said Ford cautiously.

"Oh, come, Inspector. A bogus solicitor who disappears? I'd call that highly suspicious. Not that it's any business of mine, of course."

Pulling my leg a bit, thought Ford. Probably thinks policemen never have a sense of humour when they're working on a case. He grinned suddenly.

"Shall we say, sir, that 'he's a man the police think may be able to help them in their inquiries'. That's the expression we always keep for the press." He looked at his watch. "I must be getting along. Perhaps you'd be good enough to keep what I've told you about Cooper to yourself."

"Yes, of course. Well, good luck to you, Inspector. I'm glad you're investigating this case and not me."

As he moved towards the door Ford said: "We're not doing badly so far. A girl called Katherine Walters—she's Doctor Sheldon's niece—happened to be on the river on Thursday afternoon and saw a car drive up to the houseboat."

Henderson realized that Ford was watching him closely. He

gathered up a small pile of exercise books.

"Did anyone get out of the car?" he inquired casually.

"No, but she saw someone get into it."

Henderson seemed immersed in sorting the books into the correct order.

"Have you any idea who it was?" he asked.

"We don't know," Ford admitted. "She says she saw a man on the deck of the houseboat."

Henderson added another couple of books to the pile.

"That increases the suspects to three," he said slowly. "I reckon you'll pick the right one, Inspector."

"I am sure we shall, sir."

At the door he shook hands. "It's been good to see you again, sir." The friendly note had returned to his voice.

"I'll tell Roger I've seen you," said Henderson.

He stood in the doorway until the stocky figure had disappeared, then he returned to his desk. Mortimer Campbell's exercise book was still open. "On the whole the Hanovers were a poorish lot. . . ." Picking up his blue pencil again he read on. Then he lit his pipe and sat back in his chair. He was thinking about Cooper. . . .

The next morning Doctor Sheldon drove his car to the main entrance of Rockingham College. Katherine Walters was with him.

"This won't take a minute, my dear," said Sheldon. He picked up his bag and got out of the car.

"Who's ill?" inquired Katherine.

"I've just got to stick a needle in the Bursar."

"How brutal," murmured Katherine. "What's wrong with him?"

"Hay fever. The poor chap's a martyr to it. I don't know which he hates most, the injection or the hay fever. Won't be a minute."

The Bursar was stout, fiftyish and red-faced. He was always inclined to be liverish in the morning. Touch of blood pressure to go with the hay fever, diagnosed Sheldon. Too fat, never takes any exercise and worries too much.

The Bursar eyed Sheldon balefully over his desk. "It beats me, Doctor," he said, "why you medical men can't cure a simple thing like hay fever without diggin' blasted needles into a feller."

"Well, we can," prevaricated Sheldon, searching in his bag for a hypodermic, "but it takes longer. Now, would you mind rolling up your sleeve? A little higher, please. That's right. . . ."

"Well, that's that," said Sheldon as he got back into the driving seat. He started the engine and drove slowly through the school grounds.

As they approached the tennis courts Katherine looked idly at two men who had obviously just finished a game. One of them waved to Sheldon who returned the greeting. Katherine looked at the man again and seized her uncle's arm. "That man," she said urgently. "Who is he?"

Sheldon looked at her curiously. "Which one?"

"The one you just waved to—the taller one."

"That was David Henderson, one of the housemasters. Delightful chap. Why all the agitation?"

"You mean he's a housemaster at Rockingham?" said Katherine slowly.

"That's right. Where else could he be a housemaster?" The doctor chuckled at his own joke, but there was no answering smile on Katherine's face. "Look, what on earth's the matter, my dear? You look as if you'd seen a ghost."

"I'm not sure that I haven't," said Katherine. "You see, David Henderson is the man I saw on the deck of the houseboat. . . ."

Sheldon laughed. "You must have made a mistake."

"I'm quite sure; I'd know that man anywhere," she asserted.

Sheldon took his attention from the road ahead for a moment and looked at her.

"You could have made a mistake at that distance. This is serious, you know. It means getting in touch with the inspector right away."

Inspector Ford came into the drawing-room through the french windows. He looked fresh, alert, and determined.

"Good morning, Doctor," said Ford briskly. He smiled at Katherine. "Hallo, Miss Walters."

"Hallo, Inspector," said Sheldon. He looked distinctly unhappy and Ford raised his eyebrows.

"I got your message and came round right away," said Ford. "Anything wrong, sir?"

"Well, something rather disturbing has happened. This morning Miss Walters and I were driving through the school grounds—I'd been treating the Bursar for hay fever—and we passed two of the staff. I—er—really don't know—" Sheldon broke off and looked at Katherine and then at Ford.

"I recognized one of them," interposed Katherine. "The man I saw on the houseboat last Thursday."

"One of the masters, eh?" queried Ford, betraying no sign of surprise.

"I'm sure there must be some mistake," put in Sheldon hastily. Ford waved him aside.

"You know the man's name, Miss Walters?"

"My uncle says it's a Mr. Henderson."

A tiny jerk of the lower jaw gave Ford away.

"Henderson?" he repeated blankly. "But that's absurd. It couldn't have been Henderson."

"But it was," insisted Katherine.

"Are you absolutely sure?"

"Absolutely."

For a moment Ford appeared to have been shocked into silence and immobility. Sheldon said: "When Katherine told me I didn't know what to do. At first I thought I ought to speak to Henderson about it. You see, he happens to be a good friend of mine and I didn't want him to think——"

"I hope you didn't speak to him," said Ford.

"No, as a matter of fact I didn't. Katherine advised me not to."

"That was good advice, Miss Walters," said Ford.

"You think I made a mistake, don't you, Inspector? You don't think it *was* Henderson I saw."

Ford rubbed the side of his nose. He looked worried. "Frankly, Miss Walters, I don't know what to think. On the face of it there seems every reason to suppose that it was Henderson. I don't mind

telling you that this news has come as a great shock to me——"
he broke off to look at Doctor Sheldon— "well, you know what
I think of Henderson, Doctor. If it hadn't been for his coaching
my boy would never have got that scholarship to Rockingham.
Roger owes everything to him. And now this——" He looked
almost appealingly at Katherine.

"I'm awfully sorry," the girl said, "I really am. But I'm afraid I
didn't make a mistake. It definitely was Henderson that I saw on
the houseboat."

"Of course, there may be a perfectly simple explanation," said
Sheldon.

Ford emitted a heavy sigh. "I sincerely hope so, sir. What puzzles
me is that I was talking to Henderson about the murder only
yesterday. He never said he knew Cooper."

"Did you ask him?"

"No. But it seems odd that he never mentioned him." He rose
from his chair and reached for his hat. "This is a very odd sort of
case altogether."

"Possibly Henderson went to the houseboat to see Cooper but
found he was out," suggested Sheldon.

"Possibly he did, sir," said Ford quietly. "But that doesn't alter
the fact that he must have been on the houseboat after the murder
had been committed. In that case he could hardly have failed to
have seen the body."

"I still think Henderson will produce some perfectly logical
explanation for being there," said the doctor. "It's absolutely fantastic
that he should be connected with a murder."

"I agree with you, sir," said Ford, "and I very much hope you're
right." He turned to Katherine. "I take it you're staying down here
for some little time?"

"Certainly for the next week or two."

Ford said: "I'll keep in touch with you." He smiled briefly; a
wry smile in which there was little humour. "I'm afraid you're both
what are commonly known as material witnesses."

Ford wore a worried frown as he walked away from Doctor

Sheldon's house. He was not looking forward to his forthcoming interview with Henderson. Henderson, he realized ruefully, had temporarily ceased to be a close and respected friend. Until he gave a satisfactory account of his movements on the previous Thursday he was an official entry in Inspector Ford's notebook. With the best will in the world Ford could not regard him as anything else except a suspect.

Ford's frown deepened as he got into the waiting police car. On the way home he thought briefly of his wife, dead these three years, and the motherless son who showed such promise. David Henderson alone had been instrumental in getting Roger into Rockingham. In his own time he had encouraged, coaxed and cajoled the boy towards the scholarship. Without Henderson's help Roger would probably have found himself pounding the beat in five years time, just as he, Detective-Inspector Michael Ford had done. Now, he had no alternative but to add Henderson to the list of suspects in the houseboat murder. But the job had to be done. He would have to question Henderson as he had questioned hundreds of other suspected criminals. He would check his movements, test his alibis and probe the innermost recesses of his mind with all the professional skill at his command.

But the thing's crazy, he thought irritably. As Sheldon had said, Henderson must have an explanation for his movements.

But the nagging doubt persisted. What *had* Henderson been doing on the houseboat? How could a housemaster at Rockingham College be involved in the murder of an unknown Italian?

The police car drew up outside the gate of his house. The driver was concerned: usually old Mike Ford had a cheery greeting, a word about the missis and the kids, an observation or two about the Test Match, the Budget, police pay or dangerous motor-cyclists. But today he'd sat hunched up in his seat without so much as a word. Worrying case, probably. These plain-clothes men got a bit more pay and perks but taken by and large the uniform branch was a lot less trouble.

"Anything else, sir?" said the driver.

"No, that's the lot, Barker."

"Good afternoon, sir."

"Afternoon, Barker."

The driver watched Ford, shoulders hunched, fit his latch-key and vanish through the front door. As he engaged first gear and pointed the nose of the car towards headquarters, he wondered vaguely what new headache the inspector could have run up against in the murder case.

At the end of each term David Henderson was called upon to produce a brief word-picture of the sixty-five boys in his house. Frequently, he reflected, he was kinder on paper to many of the boys than they deserved. About Stanton Minor, for instance, a flabby and spotty youth who shirked all games and was perpetually gorging himself on chocolate he had written "he would benefit considerably from more physical exercise." That, he considered, must be the understatement of the year. He was just debating in his mind whether to be more truthful about young Wentworth when the telephone rang.

Henderson laid down his pen and picked up the receiver. "Hallo?" he said.

The voice at the other end said: "This is Cooper. Are you alone?"

"Yes, I'm alone. You can talk."

Cooper's voice had a note of urgency in it. "Henderson, listen—I've got to see you at once. It's very urgent."

"What's happened?"

"I can't tell you over the telephone. Is your housekeeper away, by any chance?"

Henderson said: "Yes, she's in London. She won't be back until tomorrow."

"Good," said Cooper. "I'll be with you in ten minutes."

Henderson replaced the receiver thoughtfully. He would have preferred to concentrate upon the reports this evening and avoid Cooper and his problems which were always so urgent and distracting.

However, when he went to open the front door a few minutes later, it was even more disturbing to see not Cooper but Inspector Ford standing there.

Ford looked serious and worried. He looked at Henderson through slightly narrowed eyes. His tone was friendly but guarded. He said: "I couldn't make Mrs. Williams hear so I came straight up. I hope you don't mind, Mr. Henderson." He's got his official face on, thought Henderson; it's all the same to him whether I mind or not. Here comes another interrogation.

But Henderson greeted Ford as one man greets another when he pays an unexpected social call. "Delighted to see you any time, Inspector, you know that. As a matter of fact I've got some rather good news for you."

"Really, sir?" Ford's tone implied that he was unlikely to be receptive to good news.

"I was talking to the Head this morning," continued Henderson amiably. "He seems to have a good opinion of Roger—an opinion that I share, I may say. He suggests that we move him up a form next term."

"Good," said Ford shortly.

"Well, *I* think it's good," said Henderson. "I only hope Roger is more impressed by the news than you seem to be."

"I'm afraid I didn't come here to talk about my son," said Ford.

"Oh? Then what did you come to talk about?"

Ford sat down rather heavily. "It's rather in the nature of an official visit."

"I see." Henderson raised his eyebrows. "I hope I'm not suspected of anything. I'm really painfully respectable." He smiled benignly at the inspector but the humour of the situation was evidently lost on Ford.

"Better get it off your chest, Inspector," he suggested. "If you're going to ruin my reputation, I'd sooner know the worst at once."

"Shall we be serious, Mr. Henderson?" said Ford quietly.

"By all means, Inspector."

Ford's expression had softened a little. He said: "I've always regarded you as a friend of mine. Indeed, since my wife died you've been an exceptionally good friend."

"Well, that's very nice of you to say so, Inspector," said Henderson.

"I might even go so far as to say that I've always regarded you as one."

"I shall never be able to thank you enough for what you did for Roger."

"Forget it, my dear fellow. I'd have done the same for anyone else. Now, what about this official visit of yours?"

Ford did not answer for a second. At length he said: "I find myself in the unpleasant position of having to ask you a few questions, sir."

"Why unpleasant?"

"Last time I asked you about a man called Rocello."

"So you did. What about him?"

"You said you'd never heard of him."

"A reasonable enough thing to say. I never have."

"Are you sure, sir?"

"Perfectly sure."

Ford sighed. He said in a quiet and faintly hurt voice: "Mr. Henderson, why didn't you tell me that you visited that houseboat?"

"You didn't ask me."

Ford's mouth tightened. He was almost certain now that Henderson was holding something back. "We discussed the murder at some length," he reminded him, and there was an edge to his voice now. "You asked me questions about it and I gave you all the details."

"Now, just a minute, Inspector! You merely told me what I already knew. What I'd read in the newspapers."

"I appreciate that," said Ford. "What I want to know is why didn't you tell me what *you* knew? Why no mention of your visit to the houseboat?"

Henderson was unshakeably urbane. "What makes you think I *did* visit the houseboat?"

"Because someone saw you on it."

"Then someone made a mistake."

"Miss Walters was most definite that it was you she saw, sir."

"Miss Walters, whoever she is, made a mistake. I'm sorry, Inspector, but you're questioning the wrong man. I've never heard of anyone called Rocello and I've never set foot on that houseboat." Henderson smiled apologetically. "Very sorry, but there it is. Wish I could be more helpful."

He thought: "I've got to get rid of him before Cooper turns up. It's absolutely imperative." At that moment a car's headlights flickered across the window.

"Of course," said Henderson, "Miss Walters could have seen me in Medlow."

"So you went into Medlow that afternoon?"

With any luck, thought Henderson, Cooper will realize there's someone with me and will wait. "I'm sorry, Inspector. You were saying——?"

With his usual all-embracing patience Ford said: "I asked you if you did go to Medlow that afternoon, sir."

Henderson said: "Yes, as a matter of fact I did."

"May I ask what you were doing there?"

"Of course you may. I went to get my hair cut."

Ford raised his eyebrows. "At Taylor's?"

"Er—yes. That's right, Taylor's."

Ford slowly shook his head. He looked reproachfully at Henderson. "No, sir. Not Taylor's."

"Not Taylor's?"

"Not Taylor's, sir."

Henderson grinned. Thank God Cooper seemed to have taken the hint. He said: "Looks as though I'll have to think again, doesn't it? But I could have sworn it *was* Taylor's. That other chap always sends you away looking like a convict. I went there once, but never again. Reminds me of when——"

"Mr. Henderson," said Ford with an italicized effort at patience, "shall we be perfectly frank with each other?"

"By all means, Inspector."

"Miss Walters told me that she'd seen you near *High Tor*—that's the name of the houseboat. I made certain inquiries and found out that you didn't actually take your car into Medlow, but parked it in a field about a quarter of a mile from the houseboat." Ford looked at Henderson searchingly. "Well, am I right, sir?"

Henderson thought for a moment. He said: "I had no idea I was near the houseboat. But you're quite right about the car. I had a petrol stoppage or something, so I parked it and walked the rest of the way."

"All the way into Medlow?"

"That's right. After all, it isn't far."

Disbelief was mirrored sharply in Ford's face. "I'm afraid that won't do, sir," he said sternly, "I made further inquiries in Medlow—at the library, the post office, the cinema and most of the shops and garages. No one had seen you."

"No one?" inquired Henderson.

"No one."

"Not even Miss Walters?"

The inspector sighed. "As I've already said, sir, Miss Walters saw you leaving the houseboat."

"Either Miss Walters imagined the whole thing or she needs glasses," said Henderson unconcernedly.

Ford stood up. He looked hard at Henderson. He'll worry at this damned case like a terrier at a bone, said Henderson to himself.

"I don't think Miss Walters imagined it," said Ford quietly. "We'll find out if she needs glasses. Good night, Mr. Henderson."

"Good night, Inspector," said Henderson. "Don't forget Roger Thursday morning. Seven o'clock."

"I'll be there," said Ford. He gave Henderson a final, searching look and went out of the room.

Henderson went to the sideboard and mixed himself a rather larger whisky and soda than usual. He was just splashing in the soda when a voice from the door said: "You might pour me one, too." Henderson looked round and saw James Cooper.

Cooper was a shortish, dapper man of about fifty. In spite of his somewhat insignificant stature he had an undoubted presence. He was neat, almost pernickety in his dress. He had iron grey hair and very piercing pale blue eyes. One could not imagine a situation from which Cooper would not emerge smart, brisk and confident. From time to time Henderson wondered a little about Cooper—a process, he thought wryly, that would get him precisely nowhere. Cooper was not given to talking about himself.

Henderson handed a drink to Cooper who sipped it appreciatively. Cooper took a slim cigarette case from his pocket and snapped his lighter. All his movements were definite and efficient. "Who was your friend?" he inquired.

"That," said Henderson significantly, "was Detective-Inspector Ford."

"Oh, was it?" said Cooper. He continued to sip his drink and smoke unconcernedly. His voice, like his face, was quite expressionless.

"Did he see you, d'you think?" asked Henderson.

"No. I spotted his car and drove round the back."

"Just as well. Your appearance at that moment would have required a little explaining."

"I take it," said Cooper equably, "that something must have gone wrong."

"Somewhat," said Henderson. "Someone saw me leaving the houseboat on Thursday afternoon."

Cooper registered neither surprise, alarm or concern. He merely said: "Who?"

"Her name's Walters."

"Katherine Walters?"

"That's right."

"And she's staying with Doctor Sheldon?"

"Yes," said Henderson. "You seem to know quite a lot about the young woman."

"I know a little," replied Cooper enigmatically. "Miss Walters is the reason that I've come to see you."

"I don't quite understand, Cooper. What——?"

"Have you met her?"

"No. I know Doctor Sheldon, of course. But why all the interest in Miss Walters?"

Cooper said casually: "Two weeks ago she was in Venice."

Henderson, his glass half-way to his lips, started. "In *Venice*, did you say?"

"That's what I said."

Henderson drank some whisky and soda. "Well, that's a concidence."

"Is it?" said Cooper. "I wonder."

"What else d'you know about this girl?"

Cooper ignored the question; instead he said: "You say that she saw you on the houseboat?"

"Yes."

"But you've never actually seen her?"

"Never, as far as I know."

"And as a result of seeing you she told Inspector Ford?"

"Exactly."

Cooper looked thoughtful. "Is Sheldon your doctor, by any chance?"

"Yes. As a matter of fact I went to see him about a month ago. I had a spot of muscular trouble in my shoulder."

"Excellent," said Cooper. "I suggest you manufacture a slight recurrence of that trouble."

"What exactly d'you mean?"

Cooper said quietly, "I mean that it might be a good idea to keep an eye on Miss Walters." The thin lips twitched momentarily into the semblance of a smile. "A pleasant enough duty, I should imagine. . . ."

Chapter Four

Since the death of his wife Detective-Inspector Michael Ford and Roger had lived in a small detached house in Medlow. Ford had never succeeded in becoming domesticated and a woman came in every day to do the cooking and cleaning. She took Saturdays and Sundays off and at week-ends Ford and Roger (during school holidays) fended for themselves in an atmosphere of cheerful confusion. On Monday mornings, when his father had departed for the police station, Roger usually made himself scarce because the admirable Mrs. Bates was apt to flounce through the house muttering darkly about the inability of the male sex to do anything for themselves.

On the first Saturday of the school holidays Ford, comfortably attired in disreputable flannel trousers and an open-necked shirt, was entertaining Detective-Sergeant Broderick to afternoon tea. Ford privately designated Mrs. Bate's tea as "dish water" and prided himself on producing a really strong, man's brew.

The kettle boiled and Ford put four spoonfuls of tea into the pot. "Great stuff, this," he said to Broderick. "It'll get that nimble brain of yours working on this little problem of ours."

"I'm glad you think it's only a *little* problem," said Broderick. He accepted a cup of tea from Ford and sipped it thoughtfully for a moment. He said: "Mike, d'you know a girl by the name of Billie Reynolds?"

"Billie Reynolds?"

"Yes. She's the piece who's got the houseboat called *Shangri-La*. It's about two hundred yards from Cooper's."

"*Shangri-La*, eh?" said Ford. "Sounds like a ruddy night club."

"I gather it's used as one on occasions," said Broderick dryly. "The type that gets raided. Well, d'you know the lady?"

"I know her," said Ford. "A flash piece if you like."

Broderick laughed. "That's an understatement," he said.

"She's been questioned about this job," said Ford. "All movements checked, water-tight alibi. She was away when the murder happened: caught the 9.25 to London on Wednesday morning. Old Fred at the station remembers carrying her suitcase. Have you seen her lately?"

Broderick grinned. "I saw her last night, as a matter of fact."

"Oh, did you, now? Where?"

"In the 'Rose and Crown' at Maidenhead. I bought her a drink. Come to think of it, I bought her three drinks."

"Fancy that," said Ford ironically. He knew that Broderick was of a somewhat amatory disposition and that his eye was apt to rove. He was undeniably attractive to the opposite sex and on occasions his physical charms had paid good dividends professionally. "And what exactly was the purpose of this little get-together? I take it you were, as they say, combining business with pleasure."

"Certainly," said Broderick. "I pumped her about Cooper and Rocello. She said she knew Cooper by sight but had never seen Rocello. She said she left Medlow on Wednesday and returned on Friday night."

Ford nodded. "That's been checked. It's O.K." He shot a quick look at Broderick. "Don't you believe her?"

Broderick shrugged. "I suppose so. In any case you say she's got a perfect alibi."

"Couldn't have a much better one," said Ford. "But you don't seem quite happy about our Billie. Is there a doubt in your mind about her?"

"Well, no. You wouldn't exactly call it a doubt."

"What would you call it?"

Broderick lit a cigarette before replying. He said: "I find it a little difficult to believe that she never noticed Rocello. Granted, she was away when the murder happened, but damn it, the bloke was down there for nearly a fortnight. Billie *must* have noticed him at some time or another."

"Yes, there's something in what you say," murmured Ford.

"Look at it this way, Mike," said Broderick. "An Italian called Rocello is found murdered in one of the houseboats. The boat belongs to a friend of his—Cooper. Cooper disappears. Correct?"

"Correct."

"On the afternoon in question," continued Broderick, "a Miss Katherine Walters sees a car drive up to the houseboat and sees a man get into it. Later she identifies this chap as David Henderson, a housemaster at Rockingham College. Correct?"

Ford nodded. "Right."

"Henderson says he never went near the houseboat——"

"He went to the houseboat, all right," interrupted Ford. "The point is—why?"

Broderick thought for a moment. "My bet is he went there to see Cooper but saw a stiff instead. He was scared and bolted."

Ford shook his head. "You obviously don't know Henderson. He's not the sort of man who'd panic at the sight of a dead body. Anyway, why the hell didn't he tell me about it?"

"Because he didn't want you to know," said Broderick, with a shrug. "It's simple."

"It's not simple at all," said Ford with a touch of irritation. "I was perfectly frank with Henderson—he had every chance to tell me what he was doing there. I told him exactly what Miss Walters told me."

"D'you think she could have made a mistake?"

"I very much doubt it," said Ford. "No, Bob. It sticks out a mile Henderson was on the houseboat. And you can take it from me he knew Rocello—not a doubt about that."

"I'm not suggesting that he didn't know Rocello," said Broderick. "I'm simply saying that he was dead when Henderson reached the houseboat."

Ford poured some more tea into the two cups. His eyebrows were knitted together in a frown.

"Then what's Henderson trying to hide, for God's sake?" said

Ford. "Why doesn't he come clean and tell us what he was doing on the bloody houseboat?"

"Because he's a friend of Cooper's and doesn't want to get mixed up in anything." Broderick took a gulp of tea. "Talking of Cooper—have you found out anything about him?"

"Cooper," said Ford disgustedly, "is 'X', the unknown quantity. No one knows a thing about him except that he owns this houseboat. He's supposed to be a solicitor but he isn't. He's supposed to be a friend of Rocello's but no one knows where the hell he is." He stuffed tobacco resentfully into his pipe. "It wouldn't surprise me," he finished morosely, "if Cooper, *if his name is Cooper*, did the blasted murder himself!"

"And what about Henderson?" said Broderick quietly. "He's a friend of yours, isn't he?"

"He is," said Ford curtly. "But that doesn't alter the fact that he's in this thing up to his neck."

Broderick finished his tea, got up from his chair and began to walk up and down the room. "Let's get back to Rocello for a minute, Mike," he said. "When did he first come to England?"

Ford said: "About a month ago, according to our information. He stayed in London for three days and then went up to Liverpool. From Liverpool he came down here."

"Nothing very suspicious about that," commented Broderick. "Now, if he'd been with Cooper——"

"Cooper again," said Ford sourly. "Whatever happens in this bloody case we always come back to Cooper. I'm beginning to wonder if the man really exists."

"He exists, all right," said Broderick with conviction. "But what I'd like to know . . ."

They were interrupted by the appearance of Roger. Ford's eyes, which had become slightly fierce, softened appreciably. "Hallo, son! What are you after?"

"May I get myself a glass of milk, Dad?"

"Help yourself. It's in the 'fridge." Ford turned to Broderick again. "What were you saying, Bob?"

The sergeant said: "I was just going to ask you about that

inscription—the one on the watch. What was it again? Some bit of Latin or other——"

"*Suavitor in modo, fort* ... what the hell was it? Something beginning with fort ..."

"*Suavitor in modo, fortiter in re*," said Roger from the refrigerator. "It means: 'Gentle in the manner but vigorous in the deed.' "

"Blimey," said Broderick appreciatively, "you'd think one detective in the family was enough! Where d'you get that from, Roger?"

"Yes, where *did* you get it from?" asked Ford. "I thought you were supposed to be bad at Latin."

"Well, I'm not so hot at it," said Roger, "but that's an easy one. Mr. Henderson told me what it meant."

"Mr. Henderson? But for goodness sake, boy, what made you ask him?"

"He lent me a book about the Italian lakes and the quotation was written on the fly-leaf."

Ford leaned forward in his chair. "In Mr. Henderson's handwriting?"

"Yes, I'm pretty sure it was," said Roger.

Ford and Broderick exchanged a quick look. "Have you still got the book, Roger?" asked Broderick.

"Yes, I'm still reading it. Jolly good it is, too."

The sound of the door bell jangled insistently through the house. Whoever was ringing it was clearly agitated.

"See who that is, Roger," said Ford.

"Well, what d'you make of that?" said Broderick when Roger had left the room.

"Damned if I know," said Ford. "But one thing sticks out a mile. There was obviously some tie-up between Henderson and this Italian chap."

"It certainly looks that way," agreed Broderick. "Now where exactly does Cooper come in?"

"Let's leave Cooper for the time being," said Ford heavily. At that moment Roger returned. "Who was it, son?"

"Someone called Mr. Merson," said Roger. "He wants to know if you could see him for a few minutes."

"Ask him to come in."

A tall, spare man aged about fifty advanced warily into the room. His dark grey suit was immaculate, his stiff collar and subdued tie models of City correctness.

His voice was rather high pitched, incisive and pedantic. His hand constantly strayed to the knot of his tie. He said: "I really must apologize for this intrusion. But I'm very anxious to have a word with you."

"What is it you want to see me about?" asked Ford.

Merson hesitated and looked at Broderick. "Well, I—er—rather wanted to see you alone if possible, Inspector."

Ford turned to Broderick and just perceptibly moved his head. "See you later, Bob."

When Broderick had gone Ford said: "Now, sir."

Merson was palpably ill at ease. He looked down at his well polished shoes. When he looked at Ford his eyes did not meet the Inspector's directly. Shifty sort of cuss, thought Ford, make a bad witness. He said: "Won't you sit down, Mr. Merson?"

Merson subsided into a chair and drummed his fingers on the small side table. Automatically Ford continued to register mental impressions: bundle of nerves, probably a guilty conscience.

"I don't think we've actually met before, Inspector," started Merson.

"I don't think we have, sir," said Ford.

Merson leaned forward in his chair. He was still fiddling with the knot of his tie. "I live at Seldon House, Waverley Avenue," he said, "perhaps you know the house."

Ford nodded. "I know it, sir."

"I've come to see you in connection with the death of this Italian fellow. The word murder has an ugly sound and I——"

"It was murder, sir," said Ford quietly. "No doubt about that."

"I see. Naturally you will have verified that." Merson paused and ran a well shaped hand over his thinning hair. He went on: "It's about the murder that I came to see you, Inspector."

"Yes?"

"Inspector, I'll be perfectly frank with you," said Merson. "I saw something on Wednesday night—or rather in the small hours of—er—Thursday morning— which I think you ought to know about. On the other hand I don't want you, or anyone else—my wife for instance—to think . . ." He broke off and looked at his shoes again. Here it comes, thought Ford cynically. He might have known that sex was going to rear its ugly head sooner or later. It looks like the old story. . . .

He smiled encouragingly at Merson. "If this matter doesn't concern your wife, sir," he said, "then there's no reason why she should know anything about it."

Merson looked immeasurably relieved and conjured up a thin smile. "Thank you, Inspector," he said. "The fact is my wife's in Edinburgh at the moment so I—er——"

"Spent last Wednesday night with a friend?" suggested Ford bluntly.

Merson's smile, noticed Ford, did not reach his eyes. "Well, yes," he said, "that's precisely what did happen." He raised his well tailored shoulders in a deprecatory little shrug. "Of course, we are none of us perfect, Inspector, and in the circumstances——"

"Quite so, sir," said Ford. He spoke as one man of the world to another.

"This friend of mine is rather good at Canasta—a game I'm extremely fond of."

Canasta, said Ford ribaldly to himself. That's a new one. Aloud he said: "I see, sir."

"My wife has never cared for cards," continued Merson with gathering confidence. "So naturally I take every opportunity of—er—having a game when I can."

"Naturally," said Ford gravely.

"This friend of mine has a houseboat called *Shangri-La*——"

"*Shangri-La*, did you say, sir?"

"Yes."

"Then you're talking about Miss Reynolds—Billie Reynolds?"

Merson pursed his thin Ups. "Er—yes. Do you know her, Inspector?"

"Yes, Mr. Merson, I know her. But I had the idea that she was in London on Wednesday night." Ford smiled benignly at Merson. "You see, sir, we made certain inquiries about Miss Reynold's movements."

Merson said: "Well, as a matter of fact she *did* go to London—she caught the 9.25 in the morning—but she didn't stay there." He produced his thin smile once more. "I brought her back to Medlow."

Ford rubbed his chin thoughtfully. He disliked Merson more every minute he sat there, but he knew he must do his utmost to conceal the fact. Merson might well be a vital link in the chain.

"You brought her back?" he repeated unemotionally. "So I take it that the trip to London was to give the impression that Miss Reynolds was away for two or three days."

"Frankly, that was my idea," admitted Merson. "You know what people are in a small community like this, Inspector. One can't be too careful in—er—matters of this sort."

"Quite so, sir," murmured Ford. "Now perhaps you'll tell me what happened on Wednesday night." He was beginning to get a little bored with Merson's sex life.

"Well, let me see," said Merson, "Billie—Miss Reynolds—and I were playing Canasta and at half-past two in the morning we went up on deck."

"A rather late session, surely," Ford could not resist saying.

Merson looked pained. "Canasta is a *very* absorbing game," he said scverely.

"Quite so," said Ford. "Please go on, Mr. Merson."

"We'd been on deck for about five minutes," continued Merson, "when a car suddenly appeared and stopped opposite Cooper's place. The name of his houseboat escapes me for the moment———"

"*High Tor*," said Ford.

"Ah, yes. *High Tor*." Merson thought for a moment. "Two men got out of the car and lifted a man from the back seat and carried him on to the boat. It was the Italian chap—the man who was murdered."

"Are you quite sure of that?" asked Ford.

"Perfectly. There was a bright moon that night and I recognized him immediately. We thought he was drunk."

"I see," said Ford. "I suppose you didn't recognize the two men who were with him?"

"No."

"And what time was this, Mr. Merson?"

"Er—about half-past two, I think."

Ford said: "Do you think the two men recognized *you?*"

"I should think that's very unlikely," said Merson.

"Why? Wasn't there a light showing anywhere?"

Merson hesitated. "Well, no," he said. "We—Miss Reynolds and I—were not—er—particularly anxious to draw attention to ourselves. Naturally, a man in my position——"

Ford nodded. "I understand, sir."

"I do hope, Inspector," said Merson anxiously, "that I've done the right thing in telling you all this."

"Indeed you have, sir," said Ford.

Merson looked relieved. Then he said: "It occurs to me that Rocello must have actually been dead when the two men brought him to the houseboat."

"That's very possible, Mr. Merson," agreed Ford. "By the way, does Miss Reynolds know that you've come to see me?"

Merson looked alarmed. "Good Heavens, no! No one knows. I'm sure I need hardly ask you, Inspector, not to—er—mention my coming here to anyone. After all, I needn't have told you anything about it."

"True," said Ford. He thought: anyone would think he expected to be complimented on his public-spiritedness.

"You must admit, Inspector, that I've been perfectly frank about the whole thing. After all, some men who—er—found themselves in such a predicament might have been very much less forthcoming."

"I appreciate your frankness very much, Mr. Merson," said Ford.

"And I have your assurance that this will go no further?"

"Mr. Merson," said Ford levelly, "the police are concerned only with finding out who committed this murder. They are not in any way concerned with your private life."

Merson looked aggrieved. "I hope you're not getting the wrong impression, Inspector."

Ford raised his eyebrows slightly. "I'm quite sure I'm not, sir," he said.

Merson glanced at his watch. "I must be getting along now."

"I'll see you out, sir," said Ford.

When Merson had gone Ford went back to his chair and lit his pipe. A visit to Miss Billie Reynolds seemed to be clearly indicated.

There was an exotic air about the sitting-room on the houseboat called *Shangri-La*. At first glance there seemed to be too much furniture—deep armchairs covered with an over-large floral pattern, a divan-type sofa which looked almost too comfortable to be true and a thick black pile carpet. The whole effect added up to a curious mixture of expense, ostentation and questionable taste which, having regard for the occupant of *Shangri-La*, was scarcely surprising.

Billie Reynolds came into the sitting-room and yawned elegantly. She was an exceptionally well proportioned blonde of about twenty-eight who possessed an abundance of physical allure, a certain spurious *hauteur* and very little else. Billie was representative of a certain type of woman on the outer fringe of Britain's theatre, who haunt agent's offices by day and the shinier West End bars by night. Although she described herself as an actress Billie had never acted in the accepted sense of the word. For the past twelve months she had been what is technically known in the theatrical world as "resting". Responsibility for this enviable state of affairs rested almost entirely on the well tailored shoulders of Ralph Merson. On this particular morning the sun was shining, there was twenty pounds in her handbag and a day of pleasurable idleness stretched invitingly before her. She generously sugared a cup of coffee, surrounded herself with cushions, and lit a cigarette. In Billie's particular world, there could be no finer moment. Almost, she purred. . . .

She looked up rather peevishly as the door bell rang because it was far too early for any of her usual visitors. A hasty look in the mirror told her that, so far as outward appearances were concerned, she had left nothing to chance. From force of habit she lowered the neckline of her negligée a little and called out: "Who is it?"

Detective-Inspector Ford came into the room. "May I come in?" he inquired pleasantly.

Billie made a little *moue*. "It looks as if you are in," she said.

Ford smiled. "I'm sorry if I've interrupted your breakfast."

Billie Reynolds shrugged her shapely shoulders in an exaggeratedly French gesture. The movement caused the neckline of her negligée to gape alarmingly. "It's been done before, duckie," she said. "What is it you want?"

"I'd rather like to have a little chat with you, Miss Reynolds," said Ford. "That is, if it's convenient."

"What if it isn't convenient?"

"Then I'll come back some other time."

Billie favoured Ford with a long stare. He was quite good looking, she decided, in a middle-aged sort of way.

"What is it you want to chat about?" she said, thawing perceptibly. "The weather?"

"No," said Ford briefly. "You."

"Oh, really?" said Billie. She took a sip of coffee and lit another cigarette. "O.K., let's talk about me. Why the sudden interest?"

"You may not know it," said Ford, "but you're quite a personality in these parts."

"You don't say," said Billie, not entirely displeased. She thought she was quite a personality too. "Might I ask if this is in the nature of an official visit?"

"Mm . . . yes. More or less."

"Well, which? More, or less?"

Ford grinned. "Let's say 'more', shall we?"

"I get it," said Billie. She indicated a chair. "Have a seat."

"Thank you," said Ford, "Now then, Billie . . . you don't mind me calling you Billie, I hope?"

"There's nothing formal about me," said Billie airily. I bet there isn't, thought Ford. "You go right ahead. Let's see—it's Mike, isn't it?"

"Mike it is," said Ford.

"Well, get it off your chest," advised Billie. "Tell Auntie Billie all about it. But watch out—your third degree's showing."

"To start with," said Ford, "how long have you known Ralph Merson?"

"About a year. Getting a bit personal, aren't you?"

Ford smiled. "I'm sorry," he said, "but I did say this *was* an official visit."

"Oh, sure," said Billie. She dropped her cigarette end in the coffee cup. "He visits me twice a month," she continued with engaging candour. "He pays me three hundred a year; he's got a duodenal ulcer; and he plays lousy canasta."

"That's seems to take care of Mr. Merson," observed Ford.

"Not quite," retorted Billie. "There are a few other details that might interest you."

Ford raised his eyebrows. "Good," he said. "I must say you're being very frank about all this."

"Why not?" said Billie. "After all, a girl's got to look after number one."

"I won't deny that," said Ford. "Tell me some more about Mr. Merson."

"He takes me off his income tax," said Billie readily. "His wife doesn't understand him—they never do. Beneath a cold exterior beats a heart of gold—well, rolled gold, anyway."

"He doesn't sound very original," commented Ford.

"You can say that again. But—well—" she waved a hand round the room in a comprehensive gesture—"what would you do, duckie?"

The question seemed rhetorical. Ford said: "What happened on last Thursday morning?"

"What part of Thursday morning?"

Ford sighed. "Now, come off it, Billie. You know what I mean. You and Merson both saw the Italian and you saw two men bring him back to the houseboat."

"Did we?"

"Yes, you did. You recognized Rocello."

Billie continued to smoke composedly. "Ralph recognized Rocello. I'd never seen him before in my life."

With a touch of sarcasm Ford said: "Well, if you'd never seen him before—what was your first impression of him?"

"How d'you mean, first impression?"

"Did you think he was drunk?"

Billie laughed. "There's no 'think' about it—he was as high as a kite. He couldn't stand up and his two pals had to carry him."

"Who were his two friends?"

"Search me. I'd never seen either of 'em before."

"Would you recognize them if you saw them again?"

"Now, look," said Billie, "I was enjoying the night air and minding my own business. If some character gets fried and has to be brought home, what's it to me?"

Ford leaned forward in his chair. "I'm going to ask you a question, Billie."

"You don't say," said Billie with weighty sarcasm.

"And I want the truth."

Billie bridled visibly. "Well, I am telling you the truth, aren't I? Don't start coming the heavy copper, for Pete's sake."

"Do you know a man called Henderson—David Henderson?"

Billie Reynolds did not hesitate. "Oh, yes," she replied. "He's a housemaster at Rockingham College." Ford started. Billie said: "Oh dear, now I've said the wrong thing. Why shouldn't I know David Henderson?"

Ford had not taken long to recover his composure. "No reason at all why you shouldn't know Henderson," he said. "I just wondered if he was one of the men you saw."

"No, of course not. If he had been I'd've recognized him." Billie peered at Ford and her look was charged with suspicion and mistrust. "Here, what is this? What's all this about Henderson?"

Ford said quietly: "When did you first meet Henderson?"

"Let's see, now—about a year ago."

"Where?" Billie found Ford's suddenly re-awakened interest and penetrating stare infinitely disquieting.

"God Almighty, Mike," she said, "you're certainly turning the heat on me, aren't you? I met him at the head boy's cocktail party, of course. Where d'you think?"

The joke fell flat as far as Ford was concerned. His voice was insistent as he asked: "Where did you meet him, Billie?"

"Oh, all right." Billie's tone was inclined to be sulky. "If you must know, some of the Rockingham College boys used to come down here for a swim and I used to pop in occasionally." She looked at Ford defiantly. "Well, why not, for God's sake? It used to liven things up a bit."

"That I can well believe," said Ford dryly. "Go on, Billie."

"Well, the school didn't like it. They wrote me a letter—a real stuffed-shirt effort, it was—and asked me to 'kindly refrain from bathing while the boys were taking exercise.' Can you beat it? Well, you can imagine how that went down with me. I got myself a bikini."

"And continued the bathing routine?"

"Well, of course I did. No one tells *me* what to do. When they got the idea they got *really* narked."

"I see. And what happened then?"

Billie replied with some relish: "They sent me a couple more letters and then sent Henderson along to see me." She laughed. "The nerve of it! The saucy devil said I was undermining the boys' morale." Her voice became suddenly arch. "Would it undermine your morale to see me bathing in a bikini? I reckon it raised the little darlings' morale if anything."

"I wouldn't know about that," said Ford. "What happened next?"

"What d'you think?" said Billie with a show of irritation. "The boys don't swim in the river any more, that's all. They put it out of bounds."

"Have you seen Henderson since?"

"Once; in the village." Billie laughed. "I damn nearly gave him the V sign." She stretched herself languorously, displaying her figure to its best advantage. "Feel like a cup of coffee?"

"No, thank you, Billie," said Ford. He got up from his chair and picked up his hat. "Some other time. I must be off."

"Well, you know where to find me." She produced a smile that seemed to have a personal connotation.

Billie watched Ford's departure through slightly narrowed eyes. Then she went back to the sofa and lit another cigarette.

Chapter Five

As he lay on the couch in Doctor Sheldon's consulting room, Henderson marvelled that such a well built and to outward appearances rugged individual, should have such a gentle touch. At last the doctor turned away.

"All right, put your shirt on," he said.

He went over to his desk and found the pad on which he wrote his prescriptions. By the time Henderson had finished dressing, Sheldon was holding out the white form.

"This is for an ointment which ought to do the trick," he said. "It's not a miracle worker, but it should make a difference."

"Thank you," said Henderson, fumbling with his tie. "I wouldn't have troubled you only the pain interferes with my tennis."

"These things are a nuisance," said Sheldon, "but nothing much more than that. There's nothing organically wrong with you."

"One of my colleagues suggested an osteopath," said Henderson. "Is that a good idea?"

"Let's give the ointment a chance first, shall we?" said Sheldon. He shook his head sadly. "I know osteopaths know a number of things that are a closed book to the struggling G.P. but we have our uses."

Henderson clapped a hand on Sheldon's shoulder. "I have nothing but admiration for the G.P.," he said.

"I'm glad to hear it," said Sheldon wryly. "We are a much maligned race."

Katherine Walters came into the room. Seeing the two men together she hesitated for a moment. "I'm so sorry, Uncle," she said, "I didn't know—"

"That's quite all right, my dear," said Sheldon. He turned to Henderson. "I don't think you've met my niece, Katherine Walters."

"How d'you do, Miss Walters," said Henderson. His expression registered nothing but bland good will.

Sheldon looked at Katherine. "Er—this is Mr. Henderson," he said. "He's a housemaster at Rockingham College."

"For my sins," said Henderson amiably.

Katherine looked from her uncle to Henderson in some confusion. "It looks a very nice school to me," she said lamely.

"Have you seen it?" asked Henderson.

"Yes, I drove up there the other morning with my uncle. I thought the grounds were lovely."

"They are rather pleasant at this time of year," he agreed, and went on to dilate on the attractive aspects of the school. There was something so genuine and enthusiastic in his manner that Katherine found herself liking him more every minute.

"You're very loyal to Rockingham I can see, Mr. Henderson," she managed to interrupt presently.

"There may be public schools as good as ours, but *we* want none of them," he replied with an engaging grin. "Are you staying here long, Miss Walters?"

She was just telling herself that she must have made a mistake, that a man of this type could never commit a murder, that it must have been somebody else on the houseboat that day, when he suddenly pushed back a lock of hair that had fallen over his right eye. The gesture recalled quite vividly the man she had seen. Henderson was regarding her curiously, and she made an effort to answer his question in a matter of fact tone.

She said lightly: "I really don't know; probably another week or two—if Uncle doesn't throw me out."

Sheldon smiled. "No danger of that, my dear. You stay as long as you like."

"Do you play tennis, Miss Walters?" inquired Henderson.

Feeling like the female lead in an indifferent farce Katherine replied: "Yes, I love it."

"We might have a game sometime."

"I'd like that very much. But I'm sure I'm not up to your standard."

"Don't you believe it! Anyway, we won't have any trouble getting a court—all the boys are on holiday."

There was an uncomfortable pause. Henderson was smiling benignly while Doctor Sheldon studied the toe-caps of his shoes with extraordinary concentration. He looked up to see Katherine's eyes on him. Feeling bound to make some contribution to the conversation he said: "I don't think you've played since you've been down here, have you, Katherine?"

"No," she said. "The last game I had was in Rome, about two months ago."

"Oh, so you've been abroad, Miss Walters?" said Henderson with a polite show of interest.

"Yes; I've been in Italy for two or three months."

"On holiday?"

"No, I'm a dress designer. I've been working for one of the Italian fashion houses. Do you know Italy, Mr. Henderson?"

"Quite well. I was there during the war." As if a sudden thought had struck him he turned to Sheldon. "Talking of Italy, the murder of this Italian's the most extraordinary business, isn't it?"

"It is indeed," said Sheldon quietly.

"It's been rather embarrassing for me," said Henderson. "Someone—I can't imagine who—told the police they'd seen me visiting the houseboat."

"The—er—houseboat?" said Sheldon.

"Yes," nodded Henderson. "The one where the murder was committed."

"And did you?" said Katherine.

"Did I what?"

"Visit the houseboat." She thought: either this man's a very good actor or I must have been seeing things.

Henderson assumed an air of polite incredulity. "Good Lord, no," he said. "I've never even heard of the poor fellow. What was his name—Rizotto or something."

"Paul Rocello," said Sheldon.

"Ah yes. Rocello. That's it! I don't think I ever saw him. Of course, I could have seen him in the village without realizing it, I suppose. Inspector Ford said he was from Venice."

Henderson was interrupted by the appearance of Judy, Doctor Sheldon's housemaid. "Excuse me, sir," she said, addressing the doctor.

"Yes, what is it, Judy?"

"A Mr. Craven would like to see you, sir."

"Thank you, Judy," said Sheldon. "I'll see him in just a minute."

As Judy left the room, Henderson said in the same conversational tone: "Have you ever been to Venice, Miss Walters?"

"Yes," said Katherine, "I was there a fortnight ago."

Doctor Sheldon looked surprised. "Were you, Katherine? I never knew that."

"I broke my journey there," she explained. "I didn't want to leave Italy without seeing Venice."

"I can understand that," said Henderson. "If you ever feel like a game of tennis," he went on, "just give me a ring. Your uncle's got my phone number."

"I'll do that," said Katherine.

Henderson said: "It's been so nice meeting you, Miss Walters. And now I must be getting along." Katherine was watching him but he appeared perfectly composed. He smiled at her again and shook Sheldon's hand. "Good-bye, Doctor. On second thoughts I'll forget about osteopathy and put my trust in you." He patted the pocket in which he had put the prescription.

"Better the devil you know, eh?" said Sheldon. "Let me know how you get on. . . ."

When Henderson had gone Sheldon said to Katherine: "well, what d'you think of him?"

Katherine pondered the question for a moment. "He *seems* a nice enough person," she said, "but a little different from what I expected."

"Well, what did you expect?"

"I don't really know," said Katherine slowly. "I think someone who wasn't quite so sure of himself."

Sheldon looked at her shrewdly. "Are you quite sure of *yourself*, Katherine?"

"What d'you mean?"

"Was it Henderson you saw on the houseboat?"

Katherine met her uncle's look. Her voice as she answered was quiet yet positive. She said: "Yes, it was Henderson. I'm quite sure of that."

Sheldon nodded and started to fill his pipe. "Well, that seems to be that," he said. "What the devil could he have been doing there?"

Katherine did not answer. She was running her eye over the bookshelf. Presently her hand alighted on a book. "D'you mind if I borrow this?"

"Help yourself, my dear," said Sheldon, "but don't go for the moment. I want you to meet young Craven."

"And who's young Craven?"

"The young fellow who's waiting to see me—son of a patient of mine. He rang up this morning and said he wanted to meet you. Sounded most insistent about it."

Puzzled, Katherine asked: "But why should he be anxious to meet me?"

"He's a journalist," said Sheldon. "I think he wants to do an article for the local rag. You know the kind of thing. Fashion expert visits Medlow. What the Italian girl wears for breakfast."

"Oh, I see. What's he like?"

"Robin's a queer bird," mused Sheldon. "Clever; but never seems to get anywhere. He wrote a novel about three years ago—got good reviews too. But——?"

"Not a *soul* read it," broke in a lively voice from the doorway.

Katherine looked up and saw a slightly built man of about twenty-seven. Good looking in an intellectual way. His light grey suit was well cut but slightly shabby, and he wore a red bow tie with polka dots on it. He had the confident, slightly assertive air of a reporter accustomed to interviewing unco-operative strangers.

"Hallo, Robin," said Sheldon. He introduced Katherine and Craven proffered an effusive hand. "*How* d'you do, Miss Walters. It's so nice of you to see me. I *do* appreciate it." Murmuring the appropriate reply Katherine thought there was something birdlike about Craven for his nose was long and sensitive and quivered slightly at the end.

"Sit down," invited Sheldon, "and let me get you a drink?"

"Well, perhaps a *very* small sherry." Craven sat down and twitched up the creases in his immaculate trousers, displaying socks of a startling design.

"Would you like one, Katherine?"

"No thank you," she said.

Craven was leaning back, very much at ease, and making no attempt to embark upon an interview. Katherine engaged him in small talk for some minutes, then suddenly came round to what she imagined was the purpose of his visit.

She said: "I understand you are interested in women's fashions, Mr. Craven."

Craven looked mildly startled. "Women's fashions?"

"Yes."

"Not madly. Why?"

Sheldon, who was pouring out sherry, said over his shoulder: "I thought you wanted to interview Katherine?"

"Oh, but I *do*" said Craven fervently.

"Well, I'm a fashion designer," said Katherine. "I'm afraid my opinion isn't worth a great deal on any other subject."

"Oh, but you're so wrong," said Craven earnestly. "I certainly wouldn't say that."

"Well, what exactly is it you want to interview me about?" asked Katherine.

Craven accepted the glass of sherry, and carefully sipped the amber liquid. He said conversationally: "I understand you were on the river the day the Italian chap was murdered. Did you see anyone, Miss Walters?"

"What makes you think I was on the river?"

"You hired a punt from Barker Brothers," said Craven in a matter-of-fact voice. He sat back in his chair and folded his arms in a gesture of supreme self-satisfaction.

"Are you a detective as well as a journalist?" asked Katherine crisply. There was something excessively irritating about Robin Craven.

"Good Lord, no!" he exclaimed, as if apparently shocked by such a suggestion. "Everyone to his trade, I *always* say. Don't you agree? Although, come to think of it, I'm not at all sure I wouldn't make a very good detective. After all, I've got *all* the nerve in the world and the tenacity of a *tiger*. When I get my teeth into a thing I never let go." He smiled at Doctor Sheldon and Katherine as if the murder were solved already. "I think the doctor will confirm that—won't you, Doctor?" His very attitude challenged the doctor to do anything else.

"You certainly have tenacity to a marked degree," conceded Sheldon.

Katherine said somewhat coldly: "And what have you got your teeth into at the moment, Mr. Craven?"

Craven displayed all his tenacious molars in a wide smile. "But the murder, of course. Paul Rocello. What else?"

Katherine said uncertainly: "Of course. The murder."

"I've written a *fascinating* article for the *Daily News*," continued Craven in the manner of a man who has recently split the atom. He turned to Sheldon as a potentially more impressionable listener. "Do you take the *News*, Doctor?"

"Why, yes," said Sheldon, "but surely that's a London paper—a National."

"Of course. I'm their local correspondent."

"Oh?" said the doctor. "I never knew that."

"Neither did I until last night," said Craven with unexpected modesty.

"Congratulations," said Sheldon dryly.

Craven waved a deprecatory hand. "Well, it *is* nice to have one's talents recognized eventually."

Katherine asked: "What's this article of yours about?"

"Rocello. Paul Rocello."

"But no one knows anything about Rocello."

"*I* do," said Craven.

"And what do you know about him?" asked Katherine.

Craven passed a hand over his ruffled hair. He said: "Well, I know that he was an Italian, that he was born in Venice and that he was a great friend of Count Paragi's."

"Count Paragi?" said Sheldon, "wasn't he the chap that had something to do with midget submarines?"

Craven nodded. "That's right. During the war he commanded a branch of the Italian marines; they were called the 12th Flotilla. The flotilla was made up of midget submarines and frogmen." He paused dramatically. "Paul Rocello was one of the frogmen."

"Are you sure about this?" said Sheldon. His tone was frankly unbelieving.

"Quite sure. It's all in the article I've written. 'Murder Of a Frogman' by Robin Craven. That's not my title, by the way."

"How did you find out all this?" asked Katherine.

Craven spread his hands as if loath to take all the credit for it. "I'd like to tell you that it was the result of exhaustive inquiries and grim determination, but I'm afraid it wasn't anything of the sort. I got the information from this note which someone sent me." He took a wallet from his inside pocket and extracted a piece of paper.

Sheldon looked at the piece of paper. It depicted a frogman's outfit. Legibly written underneath the drawing were the words: "Portrait of R. 1943." Katherine took the piece of paper from Sheldon, looked at it and returned it to Craven.

"Have you any idea who sent you this?" asked Sheldon.

"Not the faintest," replied Craven. "It was pushed through my letter box on Tuesday morning. At first I didn't see the point of it. Then suddenly I remembered that the Italians were pretty hot on this frogmen business so I went to the British Museum and did a little research. It wasn't long before I realized I was on to something. I cabled Count Paragi and he replied by return. Rocello was a frogman all right—the *real* thing; Italian gold medallist and all the rest of it."

"Very interesting," commented Sheldon. "Have you told the police all this?"

Craven said complacently: "They can read *all* about it in *The Daily News*."

"I wouldn't care to be in your shoes when they do read about it," said Sheldon.

Craven looked pained. "But why *ever* not? I'm a freelance and this is a free country."

"Maybe so. But withholding evidence can be a pretty serious offence."

"Who's withholding evidence? I merely unearthed some facts that they could have found out for themselves." He looked at Katherine; his smile was almost permanent. "Now, if Miss Walters had seen something—or someone—on Thursday afternoon and said nothing to the police about it, then that would be a *clear* case of withholding evidence." He sat back in his chair and folded his hands with an air of triumph.

"I saw nothing on Thursday afternoon that would interest you or the police," said Katherine shortly.

Craven raised his eyebrows. "Oh?" he said, "but I understand you were interviewed by the police."

"Of course I was interviewed by the police," said Katherine. "I was on the river that afternoon."

"They don't usually interview people without a very good reason," said Craven quietly.

"I don't doubt you're very well up in police procedure," said Katherine. "And I'm sure it will stand you in good stead before very long."

"I don't quite follow?"

Katherine smiled. "I have a shrewd suspicion that the police will be interviewing *you* tomorrow morning, Mr. Craven."

Chapter Six

Henderson stopped dead in his tracks as he came into the sitting-room. Comfortably installed in his best arm chair and displaying a startling amount of very attractive leg was Billie Reynolds.

Clearly, Billie was dressed for a kill. She wore a black cocktail outfit, and greeted Henderson with a smile that had a wealth of promise in it. "Hello, stranger!"

Henderson said: "Good afternoon. Miss Reynolds, isn't it?"

"The very same," said Billie with great vivacity. "You came to see me about twelve months ago." She produced an alluring pout. "Now, don't tell me you've forgotten *that*."

"On the contrary," said Henderson, "I remember it very well."

"Your housekeeper said I could wait in here. I hope you don't mind."

Henderson said: "What exactly can I do for you, Miss Reynolds?"

Billie was full of self-assurance. "You can give me a cigarette, if you've got one."

Henderson offered the cigarette box to her. "You could have helped yourself."

Billie accepted a light and inhaled luxuriously. The cigarette came away from her mouth and left a generous smear of lipstick on it. "Ladies don't help themselves, Mr. Henderson," she said archly. She pulled the tight skirt of her dress half an inch nearer to her knee in a travesty of modesty. "Or perhaps you don't think I'm a lady."

Henderson looked her up and down for a moment. "Yes, I think you're a lady," he said.

"Like hell you do," said Billie. She looked at him through the smoke of her cigarette. "I was sorry to hear about your Italian friend."

"*My* Italian friend?"

"Yes. Rocello, or whatever his name was."

"He wasn't a friend of mine."

"Oh, wasn't he, duckie?"

"No."

Billie shrugged her shoulders gracefully. "So sorry," she said, "I thought he was."

Henderson looked at Billie through slightly narrowed eyes. "And what gave you that impression?" he asked.

Billie said casually: "Well, I saw you bringing him home so I assumed he was a friend of yours."

"When was this?"

"The night he was drunk."

"Drunk?"

"Yes, drunk. You know—tight, plastered, fried. That boy was certainly carrying a load." Billie produced a small mirror and with an air of complete detachment inspected her face.

"I'm sorry, Miss Reynolds," said Henderson, "but I haven't the remotest idea what you're talking about."

"Haven't you?" said Billie.

"No," said Henderson evenly, "I haven't."

"Now, come off it, duckie! You know perfectly well what I'm talking about. You and Cooper brought him home one night, or rather early one morning. He was as drunk as an owl."

Henderson said: "When was this?"

"Last week," said Billie cheerfully, "the day he was murdered. You dropped him at the houseboat at about two o'clock in the morning—he was out for the count. You boys must have been on quite a party."

"Where were you when this happened?" asked Henderson quietly.

"Never you mind," said Billie. She inspected her nails with a great show of interest.

"I asked you a question," said Henderson quietly. "Perhaps you'd be good enough to answer it."

Something in Henderson's voice made Billie look up from the contemplation of her nail varnish. She said: "Well, if you must know I was entertaining a gentleman friend of mine. I do quite a bit of entertaining, you know—one way and another."

"Did your friend recognize Rocello?"

"Yes, but he didn't recognize you," said Billie sweetly. "So *you* haven't got anything to worry about."

"Have you told anyone else about this?" asked Henderson.

"No," said Billie. She added significantly: "Not yet."

"What do you mean—'not yet'?"

Billie smiled. "I might be tempted to tell someone about it if anyone asked me. But no one's asked me, sweetie." She helped herself to another cigarette and regarded Henderson with the utmost cordiality.

"You mustn't say a word about this to anyone, d'you understand?" said Henderson. He was watching her very closely as he spoke and just perceptibly moved a little closer to her.

"Why ever not?" said Billie languidly. Suddenly she sat bolt upright in her chair; ash falling off her cigarette into her lap. "It wasn't you who murdered—"

"Good Heavens, no," said Henderson. "Put that idea right out of your head. Rocello was a friend of mine."

Billie brushed away the cigarette ash and crossed her legs. "Then what are you getting so hot and bothered about?"

Henderson smiled, "I just don't want to be asked a lot of awkward questions, that's all. You see, I'm in rather a difficult position, Billie."

"I'll say you are !" exclaimed Billie.

"Well, you know how it is," said Henderson. "A housemaster at a public school—you know what I mean."

"I know just what you mean, teacher," said Billie. The come-hither smile was back in place again.

She looked down at a set of chessmen on the small table by her side and after a moment picked up a knight and examined it with studious interest. "What's this?" she asked.

"A chessman," said Henderson.

"I know that, silly," said Billie, "but what kind?"

"It's a knight."

Billie picked up another. "And this?"

"A bishop."

"Well, well," said Billie, "we live and learn, don't we? What about this character?"

"That's a castle." Henderson indicated each chessman in turn. "Bishop, pawn, knight, king, castle. . . ."

"My old man used to play chess," remarked Billie. The change of subject, thought Henderson, had been very complete. "The old geezer used to fall asleep over it. It's a game I've always wanted to learn, curiously enough."

Henderson looked at her. "Would you like me to teach you?"

"Are you a good teacher?"

"I've had very few complaints."

Billie laughed: a happy, carefree laugh. "You just got yourself a pupil," she said.

At about eight o'clock the following evening Henderson slipped quietly out of the school to keep his appointment with Billie Reynolds. He carried a chess board, a small wooden chess box and a bottle of champagne. Taking the less frequented road to the tow-path he met no one he knew until he came to the houseboat. His knock at the door produced no response and he went in. The sitting-room was just what he had expected.

"Anybody at home?" Henderson called out.

Billie's voice came from an adjoining cabin. "Be with you in a minute, duckie!"

Henderson looked at the bottle in his hand for a moment. "Do you like champagne?"

"Do I! Just try me with some, teacher!"

"Where d'you keep your glasses?"

"Cupboard—the corner one."

Henderson looked into the cupboard. There were glasses for every possible drink. In the matter of dispensing alcoholic hospitality Billie clearly had little to learn. He selected two champagne glasses and started to open the bottle.

As the cork popped out Billie appeared in a brocaded house coat. She was freshly made up, and in a conscientious attempt to look demure had tied her hair with a red silk ribbon. This was Billie, the quiet, home-loving girl at heart.

"That's the sweetest music I'll ever hear," she said. She draped herself tastefully in a chair.

"What is?" asked Henderson, pouring out champagne.

"That cork popping," said Billie. "I didn't expect champagne. I thought you were going to teach me chess."

"All in good time," said Henderson. He handed a glass to Billie. "Skoal!"

"Checkmate!"

Henderson laughed. "That's what they say in chess, isn't it—Checkmate?" asked Billie.

"That's right." He put his untouched glass of champagne on the table. "Did you say you'd never played chess before?"

"No, never."

Henderson refilled Billie's glass. "Do you know anything about the game at all?"

"Haven't got a clue." Billie took a generous drink of champagne. "But I'll learn." Henderson observed that she had half finished her second glass of champagne.

"Wow!" said Billie, "this stuff certainly packs a kick."

"Only the first two glasses," said Henderson. He picked up the bottle again and replenished her drink. "After a couple . . ."

"You're floating on air," said Billie, turning a hiccough into a laugh.

Henderson took the chessmen out of the box and began to place them on the board. He turned round as Billie cannoned into a chair. He saw that she was swaying slightly and holding on to a chair for support. Her speech was thick and she slurred her words. "This stuff certainly *is* strong. You'll have me pie-eyed if you don't watch out. Let's start the game, teacher." She slumped into a chair and smiled vacantly at Henderson.

"Right," said Henderson. "Now, the first thing you have to learn about this game is——" He paused and looked at Billie. "Are you feeling all right?"

Billie had, not without difficulty, risen to her feet again. She was swaying dangerously by now and there was a strange, glassy look in her eyes. "Reckon I'm not," she said. She felt her forehead. "My head's going round and round. Wish this bloody room'd keep still. Always thought I could drink anything that came out of a bottle but that's dynamite you've got there."

"Would you like to go on deck for a bit?" suggested Henderson. "It's a bit stuffy down here."

"No, thanks," enunciated Billie with difficulty. She blinked at him owlishly. "Hey, teacher, you haven't slipped me a Mickey Finn, have you?" She swayed again and Henderson put out an arm to prevent her from falling.

Henderson looked shocked. "Good Heavens, no!"

"I've drunk some bubbly in my time," declared Billie, "but . . . never . . . anything . . . that . . . did . . . "

The glass fell out of Billie's hand and she fell forward, knocking several of the chessmen off the table. Henderson caught her as she fell and placed her in one of the arm chairs. Billie's head lolled to one side and her mouth fell open. As she would have phrased it herself, Billie Reynolds was out for the count. . . .

Henderson stood looking at her for a moment. His face was expressionless, but he was obviously making a decision. Suddenly, he picked up the chessmen and put them on the table, then he took a silk handkerchief from his breast pocket and crossed to the door. Having carefully wiped the knob, he returned to the table and poured the champagne from his glass back into the bottle, wiping glass and bottle clean of fingerprints, and finally putting the glass in the cupboard. He moved quickly and deftly with an absorbed air of intense concentration.

When he was satisfied, Henderson took a small electric torch from his coat pocket, switched off the light and moved over to the porthole-style window. He opened the window, raised the torch, and began to signal.

Chapter Seven

"I say, Dad," said Roger Ford.

"Well?" said his father, who liked breakfast in silence.

"What does parallel longitudinal mean?"

Ford looked up from his paper with a pained expression. "What does *what* mean?"

"Parallel longitudinal."

"Hum," said Ford. He stroked his chin and simulated intense concentration. "Ah, yes. Parallel longitudinal. Well, it means that—er—the ... here, what is that you're reading?"

"It's the book Mr. Henderson lent me," said Roger. "It says the relief of the peninsula is arranged in three parallel longitudinal strips."

"Well, there you are," said Ford. "It's perfectly simple. It just means that the—er—peninsula is arranged in three ..."

This geographical revelation was interrupted by the door bell. "See who that is, Roger," said Ford, looking immeasurably relieved. The little geography that he had assimilated at school was lost in the mist of time. "If it's Sergeant Broderick, leave us alone for five minutes."

Roger returned from the front door followed by Broderick. "Hallo there, Bob," said Ford.

"Hope I'm not interrupting your breakfast," said Broderick.

"No, we've just finished. Cup of tea?"

"No, thanks." Broderick held up the newspaper that he had been carrying. "Have you seen this?"

"What is it?"

"London *Daily News*"

"We don't have it."

Broderick said: "Well, I think you'll be interested in this particular issue. There's an article in it by young Craven."

"Craven, eh?" said Ford.

Ford opened the paper at the features page. Under the compulsive title "MURDER OF A FROGMAN" by ROBIN CRAVEN was a photograph of the houseboat *High Tor.* Ford read the article with a gradually deepening frown.

"What the hell does this mean?" he demanded.

"It means," said Broderick, "that Craven knows a great deal more about Rocello than we do."

"So it seems," said Ford peevishly. He stabbed at the article with his forefinger. "The point is, where did he get all this information from?"

"I wouldn't know," said Broderick.

"D'you think it's true?"

Broderick shrugged. "It reads pretty authentic." He took the paper and looked at it searchingly. "See this bit? 'Count Paragi confirmed that Rocello was a frogman and a member of the 12th Flotilla.' "

"That's all very fine," said Ford. "But what put young Craven on to this Count Paragi character in the first place?"

"Search me," said Broderick. "You know what these reporters are."

"Well, either this is a lot of nonsense or Craven's on to something," said Ford, "in which case he'd no business to write that article—he should have come straight to us."

"He's a journalist, Mike," said Broderick with an indulgent smile. "After all, it's his job to write articles." He jerked his head towards the front door; the bell was ringing insistently.

Ford ignored the door bell. "Now look, Bob," he said, "this isn't a case of petty larceny, it's murder! The moment Craven discovered Rocello's identity he should have . . ." he broke off suddenly—" Roger! For goodness sake answer the door!"

"Mike, you know Craven," said Broderick soothingly. "He's been trying to get his nose into Fleet Street for years. As far as he was concerned this was probably a lucky break."

"Well, it's not a lucky break as far as *I'm* concerned!" retorted Ford with vigour. "What d'you think the superintendent's going to say when he sees that article on Rocello and then reads my report saying we know nothing about the fellow? Some pipsqueak of a third-rate scribbler ..." he turned as Roger came into the room—"well, who's making all that blasted noise on the bell?"

"It's someone called Mr. Craven," said Roger. "He wants a word with you."

"I phoned him as soon as I saw the paper," Broderick said. "I thought you'd probably want to see him."

Ford's mouth hardened into a thin line. "You bet I want to see him! Show him in, Roger!"

"Now Mike," appealed Broderick, "don't think I'm trying to give you advice. But if I were you I wouldn't let Craven think he's discovered anything we don't already know." He grinned. "You can still blow your top if you feel like it."

Craven strode jauntily in the room. He appeared to be in high good humour. He said: "Good morning, Inspector." He smiled widely at Ford but there was no answering smile. "You look grim, Inspector. I hope nothing's wrong."

Ford said curtly: "Morning, Craven."

Craven raised his eyebrows in hurt surprise. "*What* a frigid welcome," he said. "I understand you want to see me about something."

"We do," said Ford. He indicated Broderick. "This is Sergeant Broderick—he spoke to you on the telephone."

Craven inclined his head courteously. "Good morning, Sergeant."

Ford picked up the newspaper and went straight to the point. He said: "I've just read this article of yours. Where did you get this information from?"

Craven was unabashed. "What information, Inspector?"

"You know what I mean," said Ford in an unfriendly voice; he was not over-fond of inquisitive young reporters. "I mean this stuff about Rocello."

"About his being a friend of Count Paragi's?"

"I mean the whole story!" said Ford. "How did you know he

was a friend of Paragi's? How did you know he was a frogman during the war? How did you know . . .?"

Craven held up a protesting hand. "Please, Inspector," he said, "one question at a time." He smiled disarmingly at Broderick. "Is he always like this?"

Broderick said: "The Inspector's annoyed and quite understandably so. He feels you should have consulted us before you wrote the article."

"Oh, does he?" said Craven with polite concern. "That's very interesting. And why should have I consulted you, Inspector?"

Ford realized that losing his temper with Craven was a waste of time. He said, with an italicized effort at patience: "This article contains information that ought never to have been made public."

"If I may say so," said Craven smoothly, "that's an unusual point of view. After all, we——" he tapped his chest, as if he was the accredited representative of the English press— "are the servants of the public."

"It doesn't matter whether it's an unusual point of view or not," said Ford. "The point is . . ."

Broderick shot an apologetic look at his superior before speaking. He said quietly: "Just exactly how did you find out about Rocello?"

Craven hesitated for a moment. He looked cautiously from one police officer to the other, then took a piece of paper from his inside pocket and passed it over to Ford. "Someone sent me this note," he said at length.

Ford looked at the note. It depicted a drawing of a frogman in full underwater kit and underneath the drawing was written "Portrait of R. 1943".

Ford studied the note for fully thirty seconds before returning it to Craven. He said: "When did you get this?"

"Last Tuesday morning," replied Craven.

"Who sent it?"

"I honestly don't know," said Craven. "It was dropped through my letter box."

"Was it in an envelope?"

"No—just as you saw it."

"May I look?" asked Broderick. Craven passed the note over to him and Broderick examined it. "What made you think this had anything to do with Rocello?" he asked.

Craven's attitude had become somewhat chastened during the conversation. He said diffidently: "The letter 'R' influenced me most; that and—well, the fact that I couldn't really think of anything else. Besides, I'd been making inquiries about Rocello, trying to find out a few things about him. When I got that note I decided to try the Italian library at the British Museum." The smile was back again; a trifle subdued, perhaps, but doggedly disarming. "A wonderful place, the British Museum, Inspector. I thoroughly recommend it."

Ford took the note from Broderick. "What else did you find out?"

"What d'you mean?" asked Craven defensively.

"Did you find out anything else—other than what's in the article?"

"No, it's all in the article," assured Craven.

Ford rubbed his chin thoughtfully. "You say you contacted Count Paragi?"

"Certainly I did," said Craven with emphasis. "I sent him a cable and he replied by return."

"Saying what?"

"It's all here." Craven pointed reproachfully at the newspaper. Really, he thought, *how* obtuse can some policemen be? "Paragi said that he knew Rocello during the war and that they were both members of the 12th Flotilla. That was the midget submarine crowd—the first of the frogmen." A sudden thought struck him, dazzling in its journalistic simplicity. "I say, isn't that a wonderful title? 'The First of the Frogmen'. I must bear that in mind."

"There's something else you can bear in mind," said Ford uncompromisingly. "If you get private information sent to you then it's your duty"—he paused significantly and with a trace of irony—"*even* as a journalist to pass it on to us, not just slap it down on paper. Do I make myself clear, Mr. Craven?"

"Crystal clear, Inspector," said Craven. He indicated the newspaper. "Do you mean that you didn't know about Rocello?

You didn't know who he was?" His smile had a hint of mockery in it.

"Of course we knew who he was," said Ford shortly. "But that's not the point."

"Then precisely what *is* the point?"

"The point is that I'm going to take care of that note, Craven!"

"Is that absolutely necessary?" There was a note of protest in Craven's voice.

"Yes, it is," said Ford. He put the note on the table.

"But that note was addressed to me. It's my property. I've a jolly good mind to go and see a solicitor."

"If you want to waste your time, that's your affair," snapped Ford. "I'm taking charge of this note for the time being as an exhibit in this murder case. You'll get it back when we've done with it."

Robin Craven grinned.

"Ah well, it's lucky I had a photostatic copy made of it yesterday, Inspector."

"Now, Mr. Craven, I warn you, if that is reproduced in any newspaper . . ."

"Don't warn me—warn the Editor. Now if you'll excuse me. . . ."

He favoured them with an insolent nod and went out, quickly followed by Ford.

When the inspector returned a few moments later, he was carrying an exercise book.

"What have you got there?" inquired Broderick.

"One of Roger's exercise books," said Ford. "Let's have another look at that note, Bob."

Ford took the note and opened the exercise book. He turned the pages slowly and finally came to an essay. It was evidently one of Roger's less brilliant literary efforts and the script was liberally besprinkled with corrections of spelling mistakes. At the end of the essay was written the stock schoolmaster's comment: "You can do better than this." The handwriting was Henderson's.

Ford then turned his attention to the fly-leaf of the book which

Roger had been reading at breakfast. Also in Henderson's handwriting was the inscription "*Suavitor in modo, fortiter in re*"

"What's that you're looking at, Mike?"

"See this?" said Ford—he indicated the writing on the note—"and this?"—pointing to the writing on the flyleaf of the book.

"Same handwriting," observed Broderick.

"Exactly," said Ford. "Henderson's."

Broderick scratched his head. "But why should Henderson send a note to Robin Craven?"

Ford said thoughtfully: "Presumably because he wanted him to know about Rocello."

"Know what I'd do if I were you, Mike?" said Broderick.

"What would you do, Bob?" Ford's voice sounded weary.

"I'd have another word with Henderson. Be perfectly frank with him. Tell him about Craven; tell him about the note; tell him everything we know—and see what happens. . . ."

Henderson stuffed tobacco into the bowl of his pipe and lit it. When it was drawing to his satisfaction he sat back in his chair and regarded Inspector Ford with complete equanimity.

"I may be a little dense, Inspector," he said easily, "but I'm afraid I don't see what you're getting at. You say that's my handwriting and I say that it isn't. Obviously, therefore, it's my word against yours."

Ford looked serious. "It's not quite as simple as that, Mr. Henderson."

"Oh? Why not?"

Ford continued: "When I suspected that you might have written the note, I sent it, together with a sample of your handwriting, to Mr. Stacey Boyd. He confirmed my suspicions beyond any doubt."

"And who is Mr. Stacey Boyd?"

"A handwriting expert, sir," said Ford. "He's been a recognized authority on the subject for a considerable number of years."

"I can only suggest," said Henderson, "that Mr. Stacey Boyd is slipping. Perhaps it's about time he retired."

Ford sighed. "I'm afraid I don't find this amusing, Mr. Henderson.

As far as I'm concerned it's a very serious matter."

"I couldn't agree with you more," said Henderson. "I only wish I could be more helpful."

"Are you *trying* to be helpful, sir?" asked Ford.

"Of course I am," said Henderson. He re-lit his pipe. "Now, then. You say you sent Mr. Stacey Boyd a sample of my handwriting?"

"That's right," said Ford. "I found an exercise book of Roger's and a book you'd lent him." He looked hard at Henderson. "The one about the Italian lakes."

"Ah, yes," said Henderson, "I remember."

"You'd written something on the fly-leaf."

"Had I?" said Henderson vaguely. He appeared to be lost in thought. "Oh, I remember now. Stupid of me. It was that quotation: '*Suavitor in modo, fortiter in re*'. "

"Right, sir," said Ford. "I asked you what it meant, remember?"

"Indeed I do." Henderson smiled. "But do *you* remember, Inspector?"

"I remember very well," said Ford. He was still watching Henderson closely. "It means 'gentle in the manner but vigorous in the deed'."

"Excellent, Inspector," said Henderson. "Full marks."

Ford leaned forward. He was clearly not amused. He said: "Doesn't it strike you as being a rather odd coincidence that that quotation should be inscribed on the back of the dead man's watch *as well as on the fly-leaf of your book?*"

"It does indeed."

"Can't you offer any explanation?"

"I'm afraid I can't," said Henderson blandly. "Even if I could I doubt whether you'd believe me."

"What made you write the quotation down in the first place?"

"I didn't want to forget it."

"You mean you read it somewhere and just jotted it down?"

"Exactly," said Henderson. "What's wrong with that, Inspector?"

Ford asked: "Where did you read it, sir—in a book?"

"Where else could I have read it?"

"I was just thinking," said Ford, "that it's the sort of quotation one might see on a gravestone."

"So it is," said Henderson. He smiled disarmingly. "And a very nice epitaph it is too. Come to that, I wouldn't mind having it on my gravestone." He looked at his watch and stood up. "Now, if you'll excuse me. . . ."

Ford prepared to leave. He said: "You're not going away at all, are you, sir?"

"No, I'm spending the school holidays here. I'll be at your disposal any time."

"I'm glad to hear it, sir," said the inspector quietly, picking up his hat.

On his way home Ford thought it would be nice if he could see the merest glimmering of light at the end of the interminable black tunnel that was the Paul Rocello murder case.

If only, he thought, I knew what the hell Henderson was playing at. . . .

Chapter Eight

Carrying a cheap American suitcase, Chris Reynolds came out of the little station at Medlow and stood for a few moments, blinking at the sleepy high street. What on earth had made Billie, his half-sister, move into a dump like this? There was no sign of a cinema, and those amusement arcades and cafés with juke boxes, his favourite haunts, were completely non-existent.

What did Billie find to do in this hole, he asked himself. The houseboat was just somewhere to sleep, he guessed. Daresay one of her boy friends had made her a present of it.

He stopped a pedestrian and asked the way to the river.

Chris, it should be known, was one of the worries of an under-strength police force and the long suffering taxpayer. He was what is colloquially known as a "wide boy". He indulged in brief spasms of regular employment and occasionally earned what is known nowadays as "good money". But for Chris it was never enough. There were the cinemas, the girls, the dances, the fags and the boozers—not to mention the dogs. You couldn't sample all these things and keep up any sort of appearance on eight or nine quid a week, unless you "fiddled" a bit here and there. Chris, regrettable to relate, was almost perpetually on the fiddle and as a result was not acknowledged as a near relative on Billie's social register.

From time to time Chris operated a barrow, ran for a bookmaker and played the dogs. If you wanted a ticket for the Cup Final, a Swiss watch, or a fancy cigarette lighter in a hurry then Chris was your man.

To look at he was not entirely unprepossessing, but the eyes were too close together; the chin was slightly receding; the mouth was weak. He boasted black side whiskers which came to a point level with the middle of his ears. His flowing black mane (which he combed at intervals of approximately twenty minutes) was heavily creamed and combed into the fashionable duck's tail style at the back of his neck. He affected excessively narrow trousers, lurid ties and thick rubber-soled shoes.

Chris's jaunty promenade along the tow-path that led to the houseboat called *Shangri-La* was the prelude to one of his occasional visits to Billie. By tacit agreement they only met when one of them wanted something off the other. On this particular occasion Billie was in need of a new consignment of nylon stockings which explained the suitcase which was firmly clutched in Chris's hand.

From force of habit—a habit acquired during his career as a bookmaker's street runner—Chris looked both ways before going on board the houseboat. He walked into the sitting-room, put down his suitcase and mopped his forehead which was damp from an unwontedly long walk. He looked round the room appreciatively and pursed his lips in a soundless whistle; Billie must be doing all right for herself by the looks of things.

He called in a nasal voice that owed much to the cinema: "Hey, Billie! Where are you?"

There was no reply. After exploring all the cabins he stood in the middle of the main room scratching his head in bewilderment. He wondered where the hell Billie had got to. This was a funny sort of do altogether.

Hoping that Billie had some drink in store he crossed to the corner cupboard. It was then that he saw the chessman. It was on the floor, partly concealed by a fold in the carpet. He stooped, picked up the chessman, and stood in the middle of the room balancing it in his hand. He lit a cigarette and grinned. Billie was a peculiar one, always had been. But chess, he felt sure, was not one of her peculiarities.

Ford paced up and down the sitting-room, smoking an unaccustomed cigarette. Just over an hour ago Roger had complained of a headache and pains in the stomach, so the inspector had sent for Doctor Sheldon.

Ford stopped his restless pacing and looked up as he heard Sheldon's voice say: "Good night, Roger." The doctor's voice was as calm and unworried as ever.

Sheldon came into the sitting-room and smiled reassuringly. "I shouldn't lose any sleep over that young man," he said.

Ford asked anxiously: "What is it, Doctor?"

"Whatever it is he'll be as right as rain tomorrow morning."

"But he was perfectly all right an hour ago," said Ford, "and then suddenly he started complaining of headache and stomach ache. Said he felt violently sick too."

"Well, he's got over the last symptom, anyhow," said Sheldon. "He's *been* violently sick. I've given him some bicarbonate of soda which should do the trick."

"I thought that was only for middle-aged men who ate too much," said Ford.

"Don't you believe it. It works on young stomachs just as well. Roger will be perfectly all right in the morning, believe me."

"Yes, but what is it?" said Ford. "Are you sure it's not serious?"

"Quite sure. He—er—went to the cinema this afternoon, didn't he?"

"Yes," said Ford. He looked alarmed. "You don't think he's caught anything, do you?"

Sheldon laughed. "No, but I'm pretty sure he *bought* something. In fact I know he did—four choc ices and an orangeade."

"My God," said Ford.

"Don't say I told you," said Sheldon. "That was a confidence between doctor and patient."

"The young devil," said Ford. "I asked him if he'd had anything to eat."

"He'd had plenty," said Sheldon, "a rather badly chosen diet, that's all. Give me a ring tomorrow if you're not happy about him." He picked up his hat and gloves. As he turned towards the door he said: "By the way, have you seen Henderson recently?"

Surprised, Ford said: "Yes; as a matter of fact I saw him the day before yesterday."

Sheldon said: "He called round to see me the other day; said he'd been having trouble with his shoulder."

"Did he say anything else?"

"Yes. He said that someone had told you that they'd seen him near the houseboat where the murder took place; he gave my niece and myself to understand that he didn't know who it was."

"He did, did he?" said Ford.

"He said the idea was ridiculous."

"And what did Miss Walters say to that?"

"Wasn't much she could say," said Sheldon. "It was a little embarrassing for both of us."

"What happened after he left? Did Miss Walters make any comment?"

"She only said that she's still convinced that it was Henderson she saw."

Ford nodded. "Not much doubt about that," he said. "It was Henderson, all right. What was his attitude when he was talking with Miss Walters? I mean, was he pleasant, or——"

"Couldn't have been more pleasant," said Sheldon. "In fact, Katherine seemed to take a liking to him."

"That doesn't surprise me," said Ford dryly.

"He's an awfully nice chap," said Sheldon inconsequently. He moved towards the door. "If I'm passing

I'll look in on Roger tomorrow, but I'm sure you haven't got a thing to worry about."

Sheldon had been gone less than five minutes when the door bell rang. Ford opened the door and found himself face to face with Chris Reynolds. Ford ran a professional eye over Chris and did not like what he saw.

"Inspector Ford?" said Chris briskly.

"Yes, I'm Inspector Ford. Who are you?"

Chris did not enlighten him. "If you're not too busy, I'd like a word with you, chum," he said.

"Oh, would you?" said Ford, "and who sent you here?"

"Nobody sent me," said Chris jauntily. "I called at the police station and they said you was off duty. So I looked you up in the phone book. Can I come in?"

"Yes," said Ford. "What's your name?"

"Chris Reynolds." Chris strode into the sitting-room and sat nonchalantly on the arm of the best chair.

"Make yourself at home, Mr. Reynolds," said Ford ironically. "Now, what exactly can I do for you?"

"You know my sister, don't you?" It was a statement rather than a question.

"Your sister? I don't think so. Who is she?"

"Half-sister, I should say. Billie Reynolds. She's got a houseboat down here—the *Shangri-La*."

"Ah yes," said Ford. "I know her."

"Well, she's disappeared," said Chris bluntly.

"Disappeared?"

"That's right—disappeared. Scarpered, vamoosed." Chris regarded Ford with scarcely concealed hostility.

Ford looked at Chris thoughtfully for a moment. A real wide boy, he diagnosed; thinks he's tough. He said: "Supposing you start at the beginning, Mr. Reynolds, and tell me what this is all about."

"I don't know what it's all about myself, mate," said Chris. "If I did I wouldn't be here. All I know is Billie's disappeared an' I don't like it. I don't like it a bit, chum."

"When did Miss Reynolds disappear?" asked Ford.

Chris shrugged his generously padded shoulders. "Search me. I got here on Saturday afternoon expecting her to greet me with open arms. An' what do I find? Sweet Fanny Adams."

"Was she expecting you?"

" 'Course she was. I brought her a dozen pairs of nylons. All paid for an' all."

"Have you been down here before?"

"No, I haven't," said Chris, "an' I ain't never coming again if I can help it. Dead an' alive flippin' hole. Soon as I know Billie's all right, I'm off."

Ford looked at Chris closely. "What makes you think she's not all right?"

"Well, she's disappeared, ain't she? Blimey, I've been waiting for her to show up since Saturday afternoon."

"Perhaps you misunderstood her," suggested Ford. "Couldn't she be in London somewhere waiting for you?"

"There's no misunderstanding, chum," said Chris positively. "Billie phoned me a coupla weeks ago and told me to be at the houseboat on the fourteenth. The fourteenth was last Saturday, right?"

"All right, we'll let that go," said Ford. "Did she say anything else?"

"No, except that she wanted the nylons in a hurry. Our Billie doesn't half get through some ruddy nylons."

"Are you staying on the houseboat?" asked Ford.

"I told yer," said Chris belligerently. "I've been there since Saturday afternoon waiting for Billie to turn up, an' proper browned off with it I am, too. Strewth, who'd want to live on a houseboat? You can't hear a ruddy thing except water going lap-lap-lap. Fair drives you up the wall."

"Your step-sister seems to like it," remarked Ford. "She's been down here nearly three years now."

"I know," said Chris. "Beats me what she sees in it—unless she's got a boy friend down here." He looked at Ford. "Has she got a boy friend?"

"Not that I know of. Why?"

"I thought if she had he might be able to help us."

"Anyone in mind?"

" 'Course I haven't," said Chris. "How would I know what she gets up to round here? But there must be one or Billie would never stick it, I'm dead sure of that."

"Did she ever mention anyone to you?"

Chris hesitated for a second. "No-o-o," he said slowly. "but——"

"Go on," said Ford quietly.

Chris absentmindedly took the chessman out of his pocket and twisted it between his fingers. "Well, I'll tell you," he said. "About a year ago I was in a bit of trouble. I owed a bloke fifty quid an' he had the screw on me. In the end, Billie coughed up." He grinned. "Knowing Billie, she must have touched somebody for it."

"But you've no idea who it was?"

Chris shook his head. "Nope. I didn't care either. All I wanted was the lolly."

"When did you last see Billie?"

"About four months ago—about the end of April, I think. She came up to town for a week-end."

Ford stood up. "All right, Reynolds," he said. "I'll make inquiries and if there's any news I'll get in touch with you."

"O.K.," said Chris. Suddenly he looked at the chessman. "I found this in the cabin," he said. "Dunno what it was doing there."

Ford took the bishop from Chris and looked at it. "You say you found it on the houseboat?"

"That's right."

"Does your step-sister play chess?"

Chris laughed. "Are you kidding?"

"May I keep this?" asked Ford.

"Sure, help yourself. If you get any news let me know."

Ford looked up from his contemplation of the chessman. "I will," he said. . . .

Inspector Ford looked straight into Merson's eyes and said: "Was canasta the only game you played on that houseboat?"

Sitting nervously on the edge of his chair, Merson said, "I don't quite understand. . . ."

Ford took the chessman from his coat pocket and passed it over. "Ever seen this before?"

Merson shook his head.

"Are you sure?" said Ford.

"Of course I am," said Merson petulantly. "Why should I have seen it before?"

"Do you play chess, Mr. Merson?"

"Well, I can play. But I haven't for a number of years."

"I see," said Ford.

Merson said suspiciously: "Look here, Inspector, what's the point of all these questions?" He pointed to the bishop. "What's this got to do with Billie Reynolds?"

"It was found in her cabin."

"I still don't know what it's got to do with me," said Merson. He stopped suddenly and looked at Ford. "Has something happened to Billie?"

"She's disappeared," said Ford briefly.

"Disappeared?" said Merson incredulously. "Who told you that?"

"Her step-brother."

"I never knew Billie had a step-brother."

"She has," Ford assured him, "and if I were you I'd give the gentleman a very wide berth."

"I've every intention of giving him a wide berth," said Merson primly. "I'm really not at all interested in Billie's step-brother."

"I don't expect you are," said Ford. His lips twitched in the semblance of a smile. "But he's interested in you."

Merson bridled visibly. "What d'you mean?"

"He asked me if Miss Reynolds had a boy friend."

Merson looked agitated. "Good God, you didn't tell him . . ."

"I didn't tell him anything," said Ford. He pointed an authoritative finger at Merson. "But let me give you a word of warning, Merson. If Reynolds tries to contact you, have nothing to do with him. Unless I'm much mistaken he's a pretty nasty type."

"Why did he ask if Billie had a boy friend?" asked Merson apprehensively. He had all the furtive, middle-aged Casanova's fear of a scandal.

"Isn't it obvious why?" said Ford. "Billie's disappeared and he probably thought she was staying with him."

Merson shook his head. "I haven't seen Billie for some time," he said with emphasis.

"And you've no idea where she is?"

"Not the slightest."

Ford said, choosing his words with care: "Has she any other—er—boy friends beside yourself, that is?"

"I really don't know, Inspector," said Merson coldly.

"Did you ever lend Billie fifty pounds, Merson?"

"No, of course not," said Merson. "Why do you ask?"

"Did she ever try to borrow fifty pounds from you?"

Merson hesitated. "Well, yes, as a matter of fact she did—about a year ago."

"And did you lend it to her?"

"I did not," said Merson shortly.

"Who did she borrow it from?"

"I really don't know, Inspector," said Merson peevishly. "I wasn't in her confidence to that extent. I don't even know whether she did borrow it from anyone."

"She borrowed it," said Ford definitely. He got up. "I'll let you know if anything develops. If Billie gets in touch with you telephone me immediately."

"All right, Inspector," said Merson with unwonted meekness. He fingered the knot of his tie. "You don't think there's anything to worry about. . . ?"

"Worry about?"

"I mean, you don't think anything's happened to Billie?"

"What could have happened to her?" Ford was watching Merson closely.

Merson shrugged indecisively. "I don't know. I—I was just thinking, that's all."

"I shouldn't worry if I were you," said Ford. "I'll see you out. . . ."

Ford came back into the sitting-room and dropped into his favourite chair. The mystery seemed no nearer to solution. He went over the principal characters once more: Merson, who was pompous and afraid; Billie, who had disappeared without trace; Chris Reynolds, who was tough, nasty and clearly on the make; Henderson, who had not given a single satisfactory answer to any question; and Cooper, who was still a completely negative quantity. Ford realized only too well that if some glimmer of hope didn't emerge he'd have a Scotland Yard officer, with an indulgent smile for the bucolic County Police, moving in on him.

He turned at the appearance of a very chastened looking Roger in dressing-gown and pyjamas.

"Hallo, what are you up to?" was Ford's slightly discouraging greeting.

"I'm thirsty, Dad," said Roger in a small voice. "Can I have a drink?"

"I'll bring you a glass of water," said Ford curtly. "Get back into bed."

"I'd sooner have an orangeade if you wouldn't mind, Dad," said Roger.

"I've no doubt you would," said Ford grimly, "and a couple of choc ices as well."

Roger looked sheepishly down at his bedroom slippers.

Then he looked up with his oddly disarming smile. Ford's stern expression softened.

"How d'you feel now, you gutsy young hog?" he asked with affection.

"Much better, thanks," said Roger.

"All right, cut off to bed now."

Roger was staring fixedly at the chessman on the table. "Has Mr. Henderson been here?" he asked.

"No," said Ford. "Why do you ask?"

"That's one of his chessmen."

Ford picked up the bishop in amazement. "This is?"

"Yes," said Roger with certainty. "I've had many a game of chess with Mr. Henderson. I know it's his because there's a scratch on it, right down the left hand side."

Ford examined the chessman. "So there is, Roger," he said. "So there is. . . ."

Mrs. Williams said: "Mr. Henderson won't be very long, sir. He's just gone up to the main building."

"All right, thank you, Mrs. Williams," said Ford. "I'll wait."

"Can I get you anything, sir?"

"No thank you." A sudden thought struck him. "I suppose you don't know a person—a girl—called Billie Reynolds?"

Mrs. Williams said: "Indeed I do. She called to see Mr. Henderson about ten days ago." There was fierce disapproval in every syllable.

"Did she?" said Ford pleasantly. "Do you know what she came to see him about?"

"I'm afraid I don't, sir," said Mrs. Williams guardedly. "You'll have to ask Mr. Henderson that." The housekeeper made it palpably clear that she was disinclined for an interrogation by the police and Ford did not pursue the matter further.

Henderson came in carrying a pile of envelopes and several books. "Hallo, Inspector," he said. He handed the letters to Mrs. Williams. "Will you post these sometime today, Mrs. Williams?"

Mrs. Williams took the letters and went out quickly, turning to eye the inspector over her shoulder. She was a woman who liked to mind her own business, and she didn't care who knew it.

Sensing the somewhat frigid atmosphere, Henderson smiled at the inspector and indicated a chair.

"I've been doing the reports," he explained. "It means wrestling with my conscience far more than I really enjoy."

"You don't experience any sense of power at being able to praise or damn?" queried Ford curiously. "Why, you might even be able to make or mar a boy's whole career."

"That's a thought that always terrifies me," admitted Henderson. "I console myself with the reflection that most of our captains of industry had shocking school reports."

He leaned back in his chair and began to fill his pipe.

"What can I do for you today, Inspector?"

Ford said: "Mr. Henderson, do you know a girl called Billie Reynolds?" His voice was serious.

"Billie Reynolds?" said Henderson. "Yes, I know her. She's got a houseboat down here."

"That's right, sir."

Henderson laughed. "She's quite a character, is Billie. We had a spot of trouble with her about a year ago. The boys used to bathe in the river and she insisted on joining them. She caused a minor sensation—or rather her bathing suit did."

"When did you last see her?" asked Ford.

"About ten days ago."

"Where?"

Henderson sighed. "Here," he said. He smiled indulgently. "She called round to see me. Why did she call round to see me? Well, since last year the Head's forbidden the boys to go anywhere near the river. Billie felt a little guilty about it and promised to behave more—er—circumspectly if we lifted the ban. Presumably she was going to bathe in something that revealed a little less of herself."

"Was that the only reason she called to see you?"

"Yes, as far as I can remember. Why all these questions about Billie Reynolds?"

"She's disappeared, sir."

"Well, I'm afraid you won't find her here, Inspector."

"Did you ever visit Miss Reynolds?"

Henderson nodded. "Yes—about a year ago, when all the flap was on. The Head sent me down to the houseboat to have a talk to her. I didn't get very far, I'm afraid."

"You haven't been there recently?"

"Good Heavens, no! We weren't exactly on visiting terms."

Ford looked at Henderson intently. His gaze was met with untroubled candour. "Do you play chess, Mr. Henderson?"

Henderson looked surprised. "Yes, I do. Why?"

"Have you a chess set?"

"Yes."

"May I see it?"

Henderson raised his eyebrows in perplexed amusement. "What exactly is all this about?"

"May I see the chess set, sir?" repeated Ford.

"I suppose there's some reason for this," remarked Henderson.

"There is," said Ford.

"I'll get it." Henderson went towards the settee and picked up the wooden chess box and board. "There you are, Inspector. I also have a pack of cards, a backgammon board, a set of dominoes and a very old Put-and-Take. Would you care to see them?"

Ford opened the box, took out the chessmen and began to arrange them on the board. "No, thank you, sir," he said expressionlessly.

Henderson watched Ford as he arranged the chessmen on the board. Finally the set was complete, except for one bishop.

Ford looked up from the board. "There appears to be a bishop missing, Mr. Henderson."

"There does," agreed Henderson. "It must be on the settee."

Ford shook his head and held up a hand to stop him. "It's not on the settee, sir."

"Oh, isn't it?"

"No," said Ford quietly. He produced the bishop from his pocket. "It's here. It was found in Billie Reynolds's cabin."

Henderson appeared completely unperturbed. He took the bishop from Ford's hand and looked at it for several seconds. He said: "I don't think that's mine, Inspector—although it certainly looks like it. Just a moment, I'll have a look."

He crossed to the settee and rummaged among a disorder of papers. After a moment he turned, holding a chessman.

It was a bishop.

"Here it is," said Henderson cheerfully. "It must have fallen out of the box. . . ."

"Well, what d'you think, Bob?" asked Ford. He and Broderick were together in Ford's office.

"Hard to say," said Broderick. "Henderson *could* have replaced it, of course, but how the hell are we going to prove it?" He looked at the chessman. "After all, there must be hundreds of shops that sell chessmen like this."

"In which case he could be telling the truth," said Ford thoughtfully. "Perhaps that one doesn't belong to him after all."

"Then Roger's mistaken?"

"Well, he could be. He's not infallible."

Broderick shook his head emphatically. "I don't think he was mistaken, Mike, and neither do you." He pointed at the bishop. "He told you about the scratch on it and there it is. This is Henderson's, all right."

Broderick turned as a uniformed policeman entered the office.

"Yes, Sanders?"

"There's a Mr. Merson to see the Inspector," said Sanders. "Says it's urgent."

Broderick raised his eyebrows and looked at Ford who, after a momentary hesitation, gave a brief nod. "All right, show him in."

"Merson, eh?" said Ford; "I wonder if Chris Reynolds has been on to him."

"Shouldn't be surprised," said Broderick.

Merson was in a state of considerable agitation. He said jerkily: "I'm sorry to trouble you, Inspector, but I—er—thought perhaps——" He broke off and looked uncertainly at Broderick.

"This is Sergeant Broderick," said Ford. "You've met before."

"Of course," said Merson. He passed a hand over his eyes. "I'm sorry."

"What can I do for you, Mr. Merson?" inquired Ford.

"I received this by first post this morning," said Merson. He fumbled in his pocket and produced a large "costume-jewellery" style earring of somewhat garish design.

"Whose is it?" asked Broderick.

"It's one of Billie's," said Merson.

"Are you sure?" asked Ford.

"Certainly I am. I gave them to her just over a year ago."

"It came by post, did it?"

"Yes." Merson took a small piece of paper from his pocket. "This note came with it."

Ford read the note. It said: "If you want the other one try Fallow End."

"What does it mean—'if you'd like the other one'?" said Merson.

"Well, presumably, it means if you'd like the other earring," said Ford.

Merson paled. "Oh, I see."

"Does that make sense to you?"

Merson hesitated for a moment. "Well, yes," he said at length, "in a way it does. You see, whenever Billie and I had a quarrel, she always threatened to give the earrings back to me." He smiled; a rather sickly smile. "You know what women are when they lose their tempers."

"And have you had a quarrel recently?" asked Ford.

"No," said Merson with emphasis, "certainly not. I told you, I haven't seen Billie for days."

84

"Do you think she wrote this?" asked Broderick.

"No, I'm sure she didn't."

"Let me see the envelope a moment," said Ford. He looked at the postmark. "Hmm ... posted in London, I see."

Merson turned to Broderick. "Where is Fallow End?" he asked. "The name seems vaguely familiar."

"It's a small creek about fifty yards from Cane Lock," replied Broderick. "The river bends at a place called Fallow. It used to be a bit of a dead end but they widened it out a couple of years ago."

"It's quite a way from the houseboats," said Merson.

"About half a mile, I should say," said Broderick.

Ford said: "Well, many thanks, Mr. Merson. I think that's all for now."

Merson crossed to the door, then hesitated, as if he would have liked to ask another question; finally he changed his mind and went out.

After he had gone, Broderick picked up the envelope, examined it closely, and said excitedly: "Mike, that's Henderson's handwriting."

"I know," said Ford quietly.

"What the hell's he up to?" said Broderick. "Why should he send——?"

Ford interrupted him. He said: "Bob listen. I want a search party—every available man on the station. I want the river dragged from Billie's houseboat right down to Fallow End."

Broderick looked a shade surprised. "All right, Mike. But I think you're on a wild-goose chase."

"Well, what do *you* think?"

"I think Billie's given our friend the brush-off," said Broderick with certainty. "It's my bet she's in London somewhere—probably at a swank hotel with a new sugar daddy."

"I hope you're right," said Ford, "but I don't think you are. I think she's dead and we'll find the body in the river."

"I'll bet you ten bob you don't," said Broderick.

"You're on," said Detective-Inspector Michael Ford. . . .

Ford stood on the river bank, looking at the body of Billie Reynolds. She had, he judged, been in the water for some time.

Ford sighed. It was ironic, he thought inconsequently, that Billie should end her life in the river on which she had lived in such sybaritic, albeit undeserved, luxury. Billie Reynolds had been hard, selfish and calculating in life; in death she was merely pathetic. Ford had seen death in many and varied forms and considered himself immune to any shock. But somehow, with a good-looking woman, it was always different.

The approach of the ambulance with bell sounding furiously cut short his reflections. Billie Reynolds was now just another complication in the Rocello case and a subject for the coroner's inquest.

Inspector Ford and Sergeant Broderick sat in a police car on the way back to the station. Ford broke the silence between them. He said: "What did Doctor Sheldon have to say about Billie?"

"Said she'd been in the water about ten days—perhaps even longer," replied Broderick.

"It's just about ten days ago that she saw Henderson," said Ford significantly.

"I know," said Broderick. He shook his head. "But Henderson couldn't have done *this*. What possible motive could he have for murdering Billie Reynolds?"

"A very obvious one," said Ford quietly. "She saw Henderson the night he brought Rocello back to the houseboat."

"Yes, but——"

"I'll see Henderson again," Ford interrupted, "and have a word with Merson. You break the news to Chris Reynolds."

"I wonder how he's going to take this?"

"How do you think?" said Ford cynically. "He'll cry his bloody eyes out, of course." He leaned forward and spoke to the driver. "Back to Medlow. . . ."

"But it *could* have been suicide, Inspector," protested Ralph Merson, making no attempt to disguise his agitation. "I just don't see how you can be so sure that it isn't." He shrugged petulantly. "Unless, of course, you're keeping something back from me."

"There's got to be a motive even for suicide, Mr. Merson," pointed out Ford.

"Yes, I know that, but——"

"Can you suggest a motive?" asked Ford. "Can you give me any idea why Miss Reynolds should have committed suicide?"

"Inspector," appealed Merson, "all this is most distasteful to me. I really don't see——"

"I quite appreciate that," said Ford quietly. "Just the same, will you please answer my question?"

"I haven't the slightest idea why she should kill herself," said Merson unwillingly. "On the other hand, I can't suggest why she should have been murdered." It was obvious to Ford that Merson would have liked to contract out of the whole business.

"That note," persisted Ford, "the one that came with the earring."

"Well, what about it?"

"You've still no idea who sent it to you?"

"Not the slightest. But whoever sent it obviously knew what he was talking about. He knew that Billie was dead."

Ford nodded in agreement. He said: "You say it's some little time since you last saw Miss Reynolds?"

"It was the night I stayed with her," said Merson. The night seemed to afford him no pleasurable memory. "The night the Italian was brought back to the houseboat."

"Was Miss Reynolds quite cheerful that night, or did she seem perturbed in any way?"

"She seemed a little uneasy, I thought," said Merson hesitantly, "although it may have been my imagination."

Ford said sternly: "Now's the time to be perfectly frank with me, Mr. Merson—I hope you understand that. If there's anything at the back of your mind, let's hear about it."

"There's absolutely nothing at the back of my mind," protested Merson indignantly, "and I've always been perfectly frank with you. If I hadn't brought you that note about the earring you'd never have found the body."

"Quite true, Mr. Merson," murmured Ford amiably. He turned as a uniformed constable came in. "Yes, what is it?"

"The gentleman you're expecting has arrived, sir."

Ford nodded. "Right, Sanders," he said. "I'll ring when I want him. Has Doctor Sheldon's report come through yet?"

"No, not yet, sir."

"Let me have it as soon as it arrives."

When the policeman had left Merson said anxiously: "Will there be a lot of publicity over this business?"

"It'll be in the papers," said Ford casually.

"Will—er—I be mentioned, d'you think?"

Worried stiff, thought Ford sourly. This'll teach him to go home to the missis every night in future. He said, non-committally: "That rather depends."

"Oh what?" demanded Merson.

"On how things turn out," said Ford. He decided to bring the interview to an end; Merson's domestic predicament had suddenly assumed a new insignificance. "Thank you for calling, sir," he said. "The constable will see you out." He pressed the button on his desk and looked towards the window with studious detachment. Merson looked at Ford for a moment, started to say something, and then changed his mind before making a dignified and resentful exit. Ford looked after him with an indulgent smile, but the smile quickly vanished when Henderson came into the room.

"Sit down, Mr. Henderson," said Ford. His voice was quite expressionless.

Henderson looked inquiringly at Ford who was staring fixedly at his blotter. He sat in the chair facing Ford's desk.

Ford said quietly: "Do you know why I sent for you?"

"Presumably because you want to ask me some more questions," returned Henderson easily. "You seem to be making quite a habit of it."

"Do you know a man called Merson—Ralph Merson?"

Henderson sighed and slowly shook his head. "No."

"Did you send him a note together with an earring—an earring belonging to Billie Reynolds?"

Henderson looked at Ford almost pityingly. "Don't be stupid, Inspector," he said. He might have been addressing a bovine pupil of the Lower Fifth. "I've just told you, I don't even know the man. And even if I did why should I send him an earring belonging to Billie Reynolds?" He spread his hands in a gesture of complete bewilderment. "What on earth would I be doing with one of her earrings anyway?"

Ford said with ominous calm: "I don't believe you, Henderson. I don't believe a word you're saying."

Henderson raised his eyes to the ceiling in a gesture of almost polite despair. He said: "Please, Inspector, would you mind telling me what this is all about?"

"You know perfectly well what it's all about," said Ford levelly. "You sent Merson a note. It was in your handwriting. The point is, why did you send it? Did you think the note would throw suspicion on to him? Or did you send it simply because——"

"I've already told you I didn't send Merson a note," broke in Henderson with a trace of anger. "And what exactly do you mean 'throw suspicion on to him'? Has something happened to Billie Reynolds?"

"Billie Reynolds is dead—murdered," said Ford quietly. "We picked her body out of the river just over three hours ago."

"But what happened?" There was no mistaking the note of anxiety in Henderson's voice. "How was she murdered?"

"We don't know. We haven't had the doctor's report yet."

Henderson said angrily: "You don't need a doctor's report! You saw the girl's body, didn't you? What happened? How was she murdered?"

Surprised at Henderson's sudden vehemence, Ford said quietly: "Supposing you answer some of those questions?"

"What are you suggesting—that I murdered her?"

"Good God, no!"

At that moment P.C. Sanders came into the room. He carried a sheet of foolscap which he placed on the desk in front of Ford. "Doctor Sheldon's report," he announced. "It's just arrived." Ford picked up the sheet of paper and nodded to Sanders. As Sanders was leaving Ford called him back: "Just a moment, Sanders."

Ford sat looking at the medical report for fully thirty seconds. Henderson said: "Well, what does it say? How was she murdered?"

Ford looked at Henderson from lowered eyelids and deliberately ignored the question. When he had finished reading he looked up and nodded again to Sanders who stood looking from one man to the other in respectful and bewildered silence.

"Mr. Henderson's leaving, Sanders," said Ford flatly. "You can show him out. . . ."

On leaving the police station, Henderson walked briskly to Doctor Sheldon's house, where Judy, the maid, told him that the doctor was not at home.

"I believe he went to Maidenhead," she said. "I'm not sure what time he'll be back."

"I'll wait," decided Henderson. "Is Miss Walters in?"

"She was a little while ago, sir. She's probably in the garden."

"Well, don't trouble her, please. Just let me know when Doctor Sheldon arrives."

"Very good, sir." Judy seemed strangely reluctant to leave. "Can I get you anything, sir?"

"No thank you, Judy."

Judy left the room, tormented by unsatisfied curiosity.

Henderson crossed the room and gazed out of the french windows, then he returned to the telephone and stood, undecided, looking down at the instrument.

Suddenly making up his mind, he took a small notebook out of his pocket, consulted it, looked at his watch and picked up the receiver. He drummed his fingers on the table as he asked for the number: "Westwood nine—four—five—one, please."

Henderson looked towards the french windows again as he heard the number ringing out. A voice on the other end said: "Yes?" The voice sounded casual and disinterested.

Henderson said: "Is that you, Cooper?"

The voice said: "Yes, Cooper speaking."

"This is Henderson."

"Oh, hallo," said Cooper, "I've been expecting to hear from you."

"Cooper, listen," said Henderson tensely. "I've just left Ford. They've found Billie Reynolds."

"Yes, I know," said Cooper in the same disinterested voice.

"You know?" said Henderson incredulously.

"Yes. I meant to phone you about it but unfortunately——"

Henderson heard footsteps coming towards the door. He said hastily: "I can't talk now. I'll ring you back in an hour." He replaced the receiver and turned towards the french windows as Katherine Walters came in. She looked at him in surprise. "Oh, hallo, Mr. Henderson. I didn't know you were here." She stood looking at him; cool, poised and mildly curious.

"I wanted to see your uncle," said Henderson rather lamely, "but I understand he's out."

"I'm afraid he is," said Katherine.

"Have you any idea when he might be back?"

"None at all, I'm afraid. Didn't Judy tell you that?" She was still cool, remote and unwelcoming.

"Yes," said Henderson, "but I insisted on waiting."

"Oh, I see," said Katherine. "Has your shoulder been troubling you again?"

"Oh, no. It's perfectly all right now, thank you."

"I'm so glad," said Katherine distantly. "Well, if you'll excuse me." She turned towards the door but Henderson stopped her.

"Miss Walters. . . ."

"Yes?"

"Have you seen your uncle this afternoon?"

"Yes, about an hour ago."

"Did he tell you about Billie Reynolds?"

"Is that the girl that disappeared—the one they found in the river?"

"Yes."

Katherine nodded. "My uncle said she'd been murdered."

"How was she murdered—do you know?"

Katherine was clearly puzzled by the question. She said coldly: "No, I'm afraid I don't."

"Didn't your uncle tell you?"

"Really, Mr. Henderson," her voice was now remote. "Doctor Sheldon doesn't discuss his patients with me."

"Was Miss Reynolds a patient of his, then?"

"She may have been, I'm not sure. The police surgeon is away at the moment. That's why my uncle was called in." Curiosity overrode coldness. "Is that why you wanted to see my uncle, because of what's happened to Miss Reynolds?"

"Yes," answered Henderson quietly. "I want to know how she was murdered."

"Was Billie Reynolds a friend of yours?"

"No."

"Then why are you so interested in her?"

Henderson smiled briefly. "For a number of reasons," he said, "but I'll give you just one—the most important one. The police think I murdered her."

"And did you?" she asked simply.

"No. Strange as it may seem, I'm not in the habit of murdering people."

"Then why should the police suspect you?"

"Because they think that this murder may be tied up with the other one—Paul Rocello's."

"I see," said Katherine thoughtfully.

Henderson looked at her quizzically. "I wonder if you do see, Miss Walters."

Katherine said: "Look, Mr. Henderson, do you mind if I ask you a very frank question?"

"Not at all."

"You remember the time you came here to see my uncle because your shoulder was hurting?"

"Yes?"

"Was your shoulder really hurting, or was it just an excuse to come here?"

Henderson thought for a moment. "It was just an excuse," he said at length. "I knew you'd reported me to the police and I wanted to take a good look at you."

"That's not what you said at the time," retorted Katherine; "you said that you knew someone had reported you, but you didn't know who that someone was."

"I didn't want to embarrass you."

"Oh, really?" said Katherine coolly. She looked straight at him. Very blue, those eyes were, and very candid. "It *was* you I saw that afternoon, wasn't it?"

"No," said Henderson steadily, "it wasn't."

"But it *was*," insisted Katherine. "I saw you quite distinctly. I saw you leave the houseboat and get into the car."

Henderson shook his head. "Sorry," he said apologetically. "It might have been someone who looked like me—obviously it was—but I assure you it wasn't me."

Katherine stared at Henderson for a moment and then moved away. Her silence spoke volumes of disbelief. The uncomfortable silence between them was broken by the appearance of Doctor Sheldon. He looked at Henderson and said: "Oh, hallo—hope you haven't been waiting long."

"No," said Henderson, "not very long. . . ."

Sheldon turned to Katherine. "Did Nurse Steele telephone?"

"Yes. Judy took the call; there's a message on your desk."

"Oh, good," said Sheldon.

"Would you like a cup of tea?"

"Er—later, Katherine." Sheldon put his instrument bag on the settee and looked at Henderson again.

"Did you have an appointment?"

"No, I'm afraid I didn't," replied Henderson. "I wanted to see you about Billie Reynolds." As Sheldon raised his eyebrows, he said: "Inspector Ford told me that it was you that examined the body."

"That's right. I'm doing the police surgeon's job while he's away."

"Exactly how did she die?"

"She was murdered," said Sheldon quietly, looking across at Katherine.

"I know that. But how?"

"You say you've seen Inspector Ford?"

"Yes, I've just left him. It was Ford that told me about the murder in the first place."

"Then why didn't you ask Inspector Ford your question?" Sheldon spoke bluntly.

Henderson shrugged. "Well, I thought you'd know more about it, that's all. You're the doctor."

"Exactly," said Sheldon. "I've made my report and as far as I'm concerned it's confidential. If you've got any questions to ask, ask Inspector Ford."

"All right, Doctor," said Henderson. "Sorry to have bothered you."

Obviously puzzled at Henderson's curiosity, which seemed both out of character and in questionable taste, Sheldon acknowledged the apology with a rather frigid inclination of his head. A change of subject seemed clearly indicated. "By the way," he remarked, "how's that shoulder of yours?"

"Much better, thanks," Henderson said. "I've even started to play tennis again. I think your ointment did the trick."

"I thought it would," said Sheldon.

When Henderson had gone Sheldon stood for a moment, frowning after him. He wondered what had occasioned Henderson's seemingly morbid and unhealthy interest in the death of Billie Reynolds. . . .

Chapter Nine

Mrs. Williams wrinkled her nostrils in distaste as she regarded Chris Reynolds who was lounging elegantly in Henderson's best armchair. She stood, hands on hips, and contemplated him as one who looks upon a bad egg at close range. Relaxed, and apparently without a care in the world, Chris was carrying out running repairs on his finger-nails with a pocket file. He offended Mrs. Williams's eyes and she was at considerable pains to let him know it.

Mrs. Williams wondered sadly what things were coming to. She was the last person to think ill of the dead but one of Mr. Henderson's other visitors had clearly been no better than she should be and had ended up drowned in the river. And now this young man with the pasty face and over-brilliantined head (which had already made an unpleasant mark on the armchair) had made himself at home, as casual as you please. Mrs. Williams sighed audibly and in the sigh was disapproval and an over-current of dislike. She said curtly: "Mr. Henderson's just arrived."

Chris Reynolds pushed tenaciously at an errant cuticle before answering. He then looked up and met Mrs. Williams's grim scrutiny with a winning smile.

"Told you he wouldn't be long, ma," he said.

"You've been here over half an hour," Mrs. Williams told him, as if every second had shortened her life.

Henderson came into the room and stopped dead when he saw Reynolds. Mrs. Williams shot him a meaning glance. "A gentleman to see you, sir," she said with crushing disdain, and sailed out of the room. There was fierce resentment in every step.

"Who are you?" inquired Henderson.

"Are you Henderson?"

"Yes. What do you want?"

Chris grinnned and held out his hand. "Pleased to meet you. Reynolds is the name. Chris Reynolds."

Henderson did not shake hands. "Yes?" he said curtly.

Chris remained unaffected by Henderson's curtness. "Doesn't the name Reynolds mean nothing to you?"

Henderson said: "Reynolds, eh?"

"S'right, mate. Christopher Hubert Reynolds. My friends call me Chris." He lit a cigarette and inhaled with pleasure.

"Was Miss—Billie Reynolds a relation of yours?"

"Sure," said Chris. "She was my sister."

"I'm sorry," said Henderson, "I didn't realize that. I was very sorry to hear about your sister."

Reynolds waved the sympathy aside with an airy gesture. "Sad, ain't it?" he said. He looked anything but sad about it. "Very, very sad. Mind you," he went on judicially, "I always said she'd come to a sticky end. You can't play with fire an' not get burnt, can you, Mr. Henderson?" He smiled, but the smile did not reach his eyes: "Or can you?"

"What exactly is it you want?" asked Henderson.

Chris flicked ash on to the carpet and passed a hand over his greasy mane. "I just wanted to have a little friendly chat, that's all. I knew you was a friend of Billie's and so——"

"Who told you I was a friend of your sister's?" broke in Henderson. He sat down on the arm of the settee and watched Reynolds closely.

"Billie did," replied Chris, "said some very nice things about you an' all. 'Mr. Henderson's different,' she says, 'he's such a *gentleman*.' Very partial to the public school type was my sister. Funny really, considering."

"There seems to be some mistake," said Henderson quietly. "I only met your sister once and that was twelve months ago."

"Oh, is that so?" said Reynolds in what he imagined to be a heavily sarcastic tone. "Maybe your memory ain't as good as it was. Have you forgotten the time she came here?"

"When was that?" asked Henderson cautiously.

"S'posing you tell me?" countered Chris amiably. He got up from his chair and faced Henderson. The smile was still in position. "Well, when was it, chum? Just over a week ago?"

Henderson said casually: "Are you by any chance trying to blackmail me?"

Chris registered horror at such an insinuation. "What, blackmail you?" he said, "the very idea! You was a friend of Billie's, Mr. Henderson, an' any friend of Billie's is a friend of mine, get it?"

"I'm beginning to," said Henderson shortly.

"If you must know," continued Chris expansively, "I feel very friendly disposed towards you, very friendly."

"I'm delighted to hear it," said Henderson. He regarded Chris with a mixture of amusement and distaste. "I've met your type before. You're up to something. I'd like to know what."

"Can you play chess?" asked Chris.

Henderson sprang across the room and seized Reynolds by the lapels of his jacket. His mouth was set as he held Chris in a vice-like grip. Chris's eyes widened in fear.

"I asked you what you were up to, Reynolds," he said, ominously quiet. "Now tell me."

Chris shook himself free from Henderson's grasp and straightened his coat. His veneer of toughness was back and the ingratiating smile had turned into a sneer. He said: "Want to know something, chum? My sister kept a diary, see, a nice chatty day-to-day diary. Well, it so happens yours truly found that diary"—Chris paused dramatically so that his words would take effect—"I found it at the bottom of an old chest-of-drawers." He pointed a finger at Henderson. "Know what, mate? You're in that diary and so are a hell of a lot of other people."

"Well?" said Henderson.

"Use your imagination, teacher," said Reynolds insolently.

Henderson contemplated Reynolds thoughtfully for a moment. Chris lit another cigarette with an air of complete detachment. Henderson said: "Where is this diary?"

"Wouldn't you like to know?" said Chris in tones of bitterest contempt. "Think I'm a sucker? D'you think I carry it around with me? Use your loaf, for Gawd's sake."

"I'm serious," said Henderson quietly. "Where is it?"

"How much?" sneered Reynolds.

"I don't quite understand," said Henderson. "What d'you mean 'how much'?"

"Don't give me that," said Reynolds viciously. "You know bloody well what I mean. That diary's worth lolly, mate—a nice packet of lolly. Now then, how much?"

Henderson shrugged. "How can I tell you what it's worth when I haven't seen it?"

Reynolds looked at Henderson through narrowed eyes. After a moment he said: "O.K., chumsey. You can see it tonight. Meet me at the houseboat at seven o'clock."

"Now, just a minute," said Henderson in a conciliatory voice, "has anyone else seen this diary—have you shown it to anyone else?"

"What d'you take me for?"

"Are you sure?"

"Course I'm sure."

"All right," said Henderson levelly. "I'll come and see you at seven o'clock."

Reynolds looked at Henderson suspiciously. "And no tricks, mind."

"Don't be a bigger fool than God made you, Reynolds," said Henderson curtly.

Chris twisted his mouth into a leer. He's coming out with something straight from Hollywood now, thought Henderson wearily. He was not disappointed.

"Don't ever do that again, Mr. Henderson," said Chris menacingly.

"Do what again?"

Reynolds hunched his shoulders in a gesture of distaste. "Don't catch hold of me like that again. I don't like it, mate. I've always been allergic to that sorta thing." His hand suddenly went to his pocket and brought out a knife. He flicked open the blade expertly. "You took an awful risk, teacher."

Henderson came to the conclusion that he was rather tired of Christopher Hubert Reynolds. He moved very quickly. His left hand closed on Chris's wrist and pressed gently. Chris Reynolds struggled and started to sweat.

"I'll tell you something I'm allergic to," said Henderson, scarcely more than conversationally; "I'm allergic to silly little men with knives." His grip relaxed a little. "Now, put that thing away and don't be stupid."

Chris sized up Henderson with a wary and professional eye. Then he put the knife back in his pocket. He groped in his mind for a crushing rejoinder, but failed to find one good enough. He finally settled for: "O.K., teacher, O.K...." He dusted his coat down, squared his shoulders, shot a final venomous look at Henderson and went out. Henderson stood looking after him for a moment and then moved quickly over to the telephone.

He said, with a note of urgency in his voice: "Get me Westwood 9451...."

Chapter Ten

Inspector Ford was reading yet another report. At the rate the paper's piling up on this case, he thought sourly, it'll need a filing cabinet all to itself. Sergeant Broderick came into the office. " 'Morning, Mike," he said. Ford looked up from his desk and grunted.

Broderick looked at Ford for a moment, weighing up his mood. "Did you know young Craven was outside?"

Ford put the report down and nodded. "Yes, I know. I've refused to see him."

"Why?" queried Broderick.

"Because I don't want to see any newspaper men," said Ford, "and young Craven least of all." He regarded Broderick with suspicion tinged with disapproval. "And where the hell have you been all day?"

"I went over to Slough to interview a woman," said Broderick airily.

"Fancy that, now," said Ford with weighty irony. "May I know who she was and why you were interviewing her?"

"Sure," said Broderick. "She's a woman in Slough who was supposed to be a friend of Billie Reynolds. It turned out she'd never even seen her."

Ford smiled sardonically. "Who put you on to her?"

"Chris Reynolds," said Broderick distastefully.

"Ah," said Ford thoughtfully; "one of these days I'm going to do something rather drastic about that young man. By the way, did you break the news to him?"

"Yes," said Broderick. "He was heart-broken—I don't think. I might have been talking about a stranger. He never batted an eye-lid."

"Wasn't he surprised?"

"Didn't seem to be. Apparently he always knew his sister would come to a sticky end."

"He's a charmer, that young man," said Ford grimly. "A real charmer."

"I'm not sure friend Reynolds doesn't know a great deal more about this business than we think he does," said Broderick.

"Why do you say that?"

Broderick shrugged. "Just a hunch of mine."

Ford said: "You could be right at that. Have another talk to Reynolds. Drop in on him tonight sometime; he won't be expecting you."

"He wasn't expecting me this morning but it didn't seem to worry him a hell of a lot." Broderick perched himself on the arm of a chair facing Ford's desk. "By the way, has a Miss Rocello phoned you?"

"She called about an hour ago," replied Ford. He looked at his watch. "I'm seeing her at six o'clock."

"She's Paul Rocello's sister," went on Broderick; "she arrived in Medlow this afternoon. Apparently she's staying at the White Hart."

"I know that," said Ford. He shot a suspicious look at Broderick. "How did *you* know?"

Broderick grinned. "I'm a detective," he said simply. "As a matter of fact, I bumped into Ted Crawford, the head porter. He tipped me off. What's she doing in Medlow, Mike?"

"She didn't say. Just told me who she was and said she wanted to see me."

Broderick examined his finger-nails with an air of studious detachment. "According to Ted she's quite a dish."

"I don't know what you mean, Sergeant," said Ford primly. He looked at Broderick meaningly. "She'll be here any minute now and she's coming to see *me*."

Broderick grinned and took the hint. P.C. Sanders came into the office as Broderick moved to the door. "Miss Rocello to see you, sir," he announced.

"O.K.," said Broderick casually, "want me to go?"

"No, you can stay," said Ford, "but remember—this is strictly business, understand?"

Broderick looked puzzled. "What d'you mean?"

"I mean," said Ford, choosing his words with care, "that there will be no opportunities for exercising the Broderick charm, follow me?"

"I follow," said Broderick meekly. At that moment P.C. Sanders came into the office.

"Miss Rocello is here now, sir," he said.

Ford said: "Remember what I said, Bob. All right, show her in, Sanders."

Maria Rocello came as something of a shock to Ford. Knowing little of Italian women, he had expected a stoutish, voluble, somewhat blowsy woman with an olive complexion. Maria Rocello was, in fact, somewhere in her late twenties and was neither stout, voluble, blowsy or olive-complexioned. She was tall, beautiful and poised. There was about her an almost Madonna-like quality. She had black hair, an almost dead white face, red lips and dark, expressive eyes. Ford thought that Broderick's description "quite a dish" was apt enough; it was almost impossible for any man to be unmoved at the appearance of Maria Rocello.

Ford said pleasantly: "Miss Rocello? I'm Detective-Inspector Ford." She smiled and extended a slim, white hand. "This is my assistant, Detective-Sergeant Broderick."

Her voice was low, tuneful and practically accentless. She said: "How d'you do? It's very kind of you to see me at such short notice."

"Do sit down," said Ford. He offered his cigarette case but she refused.

Ford sat down behind his desk. He noticed that Broderick was eyeing Maria Rocello with scarcely veiled appreciation. He said: "You said over the telephone that you'd just arrived from Italy, Miss Rocello."

She inclined her head. Her every movement was imbued with subtle grace. She said: "Yes, I left Milan this morning at seven o'clock."

"I'm curious to know why you came to Medlow," said Ford. "If it's information you want surely Scotland Yard would have been the best place."

"I did go to Scotland Yard," said Maria Rocello. "I saw a Superintendent Harringay. He told me you were in charge of the case." Suddenly her voice became tense and concerned. She said: "Inspector, why was my brother murdered?"

"I'm afraid we don't know why, Miss Rocello," said Ford. "We're still pursuing our investigations."

"But you must have some—some—*idea* as to why this terrible thing has happened," she persisted.

"Have *you* any idea why it happened, Miss Rocello?" asked Broderick quietly.

"Why, no," she said at once. "When I heard the news I could hardly believe it. I thought at first there had been some mistake."

Ford had been gazing thoughtfully at his blotter. He paused in the middle of drawing a ship and asked: "Can you tell me something about this man Cooper, Miss Rocello? Was he a very good friend of your brother?"

"They seemed to be good friends," said Maria. "Paul introduced me to him about two years ago. Is it true that Mr. Cooper's disappeared?"

"It's true, Miss Rocello," said Broderick.

Ford looked at Maria and then opened a drawer in his desk. From it he took the wristlet watch which had been found on the murdered man. He held up the watch so that the dial faced Maria. He said: "Miss Rocello, have you ever seen this watch before?"

She said unhesitatingly: "But of course. It's Paul's."

"There's an inscription on the back," said Ford.

"That's right," said Maria. "It is our family"—she hesitated for a moment.

"Motto?" suggested Ford.

Maria smiled apologetically. "My English is quite good most of

103

the time," she said, "but occasionally I am lost for a word. You have supplied the word I was looking for, Inspector. Family motto is right."

"In English it means 'gentle in the manner but vigorous in the deed'," said Ford. "Is that right, Miss Rocello?"

Maria smiled and nodded. "Quite right, Inspector."

Ford sat looking at the watch for a moment. Then he put it down on his desk and leaned forward. "Miss Rocello," he said, "did your brother ever mention a man called David Henderson?"

Maria's forehead puckered in a frown. "David Henderson?"

"Yes."

"No," she said slowly, "I never heard that name before."

"You're sure?"

She nodded emphatically. "Quite sure. Who is he?"

Ford said: "He's a schoolmaster at a public school near Medlow. We think he might be concerned, in some way or other, with the death of your brother."

"What do you mean?" asked Maria quickly. Her voice had lost some of its quiet and well modulated timbre. "Did he murder my brother?"

"We don't know who murdered your brother, Miss Rocello," replied Ford quietly.

"But you think this man Henderson——"

"We're not quite sure about Henderson," broke in Ford. "We're still making inquiries."

Maria looked from Ford to Broderick but they both wore blank, official faces; devoid of expression. "I see," she said softly.

Broderick said: "I assure you we're doing everything we can. We're just as anxious to find the murderer as you are, Miss Rocello."

She inclined her head gracefully. "I realize that, of course," she said.

"How long do you propose staying in Medlow?" asked Ford.

"Until something definite happens," said Maria decisively. "I shall stay until you make an arrest or decide that the case is over."

"A murder case is never *over*, as you put it," pointed out Ford, "until we've arrested the murderer." He smiled ruefully. "Sometimes they take years to solve. There's really no reason why you should stay, you know. We can always get in touch with you."

"I shall stay," she said composedly, "for a time, at any rate."

Ford got up from his chair. "All right, Miss Rocello," he said, "it's entirely up to you, of course. If you want us, you know where we are. And thank you for calling."

Maria, too, rose to her feet. "Thank you, Inspector."

"If anyone contacts you," went on Ford, "let me know at once, please."

She said: "But I don't know anyone in Medlow. Do you mean newspaper men—reporters?"

"I mean anyone," said Ford. "Whoever contacts you, let me know."

"Why, yes, Inspector," said Maria Rocello. She looked uncertainly at Ford.

"Believe me, Miss Rocello," said Ford, "I have a reason for asking."

"Very well," she said. She smiled at the two men and left the office.

A few minutes later Broderick left and Ford studied the wrist watch intently. The hands registered a quarter past six. . . .

The hands on Henderson's wrist watch pointed to five minutes to seven as he crossed the tow-path leading to the houseboat *Shangri-La*. Getting Billie's diary from Chris Reynolds, he thought, might present certain problems.

Chris was lounging in the armchair listening to the radio and snapping his fingers to the strains of a rhumba. With a lordly gesture he indicated that Henderson should sit down.

"Make yourself at home, teacher," he invited. He exuded an oily *bonhomie* that Henderson found both irritating and vaguely disquieting. He thought: this may be a bit tougher than I expected.

Henderson stood looking at Chris for a moment. Chris's expression registered bland good-will. "Well, come on," he said, "take the weight off your feet." He pushed a cigarette box across the table. "Have a fag."

"No thanks," said Henderson. At Reynolds's elbow he noticed a leather-covered book which he took to be Billie's diary.

"Not very chatty, are we?" said Chris. He leaned back to twiddle the knob of the wireless and the rhumba reverberated through the room.

Henderson said: "I think you know what I've come for, Reynolds."

"Sure," said Chris. He indicated the diary. "You've come for this."

"That's right," said Henderson. He held out his hand. "I'll take it now, if you don't mind. I'm in rather a hurry."

Chris's eyes narrowed. "Just a minute, teacher," he said. "What about the lolly?"

"The lolly?"

"Don't come the sixth-form stuff with me, chum," said Chris. "You know ruddy well what I mean. I told you this diary"—he patted it in a proprietorial way—"was worth a nice little packet. Lolly means money, see? You know—scratch, pertaters, cabbage. What you think it's worth, teacher?"

"I think you've got the wrong idea," said Henderson quietly.

"I haven't, y'know," said Chris. "Now, let's see. I reckon it's worth five 'undred nicker. That's what I call a nice, reasonable price." He gestured with his hand. "You hand over the five hundred an' I hand over the diary. Fair enough?"

Henderson shook his head. "Sorry, Reynolds," he said, "I'm afraid I haven't come here to *buy* the diary. Now, if you don't mind, I'll take it." He reached out a hand towards the table.

Reynolds was on his feet in an instant. His hand went to his pocket and he produced the flick knife that Henderson had seen earlier. He pressed the catch and the blade shot out. "Oh, no," he said, "that's not the idea at all. No money, no diary."

Henderson sighed. "You know, Reynolds," he said, "you're being very stupid about this."

"Think so?" said Chris. He waved the knife gently from side to side.

"Yes, I do," said Henderson. He moved a little closer to Reynolds. His hands hung loosely by his sides. "I told you before I don't much care for young men with knives."

" 'I don't much care for young men with knives',￼" mimicked Reynolds savagely. "What you going to do about it, teacher?"

"I know what I'd like to do," said Henderson quietly. "I'd like to bend you over and give you six of the best." Before the words were out of his mouth he grabbed the cloth off the table and threw it in Reynolds's face. At the same time he made a grab for his other hand.

Henderson was quick but not quite quick enough. The blade of the knife slashed across the back of his hand as he closed with Reynolds. Henderson drew back his left fist and planted it squarely in Chris's midriff. As Chris doubled up Henderson brought his right hand down with a chopping motion on Reynolds's wrist. The knife clattered to the floor and Henderson put his foot on it.

"The diary, please," said Henderson.

"You bastard!" hissed Reynolds. He lashed out with his uninjured hand. Henderson took the blow on his forearm and drove a short, driving right-hander to Chris's jaw. Chris went down and stayed down.

Henderson stood, rubbing his knuckles, looking at Chris Reynolds. He felt the blood from his cut hand trickling down his fingers. Then he picked up the diary. . . .

Obviously a desperate struggle had taken place in the sitting-room of the houseboat called *Shangri-La*. From the overturned table to the scattered chairs the scene was one of wild disorder.

Robin Craven received no answer to his knock at the door and went in. He stood in the middle of the room, looking about him in bewilderment. He jumped suddenly at the sound of a voice behind him. "Good evening, Mr. Craven. This is a pleasant surprise." Craven looked round guiltily. Dectective-Sergeant Broderick was leaning indolently against the door. His attitude was relaxed, slightly mocking and watchful.

"What are you doing here?" demanded Craven.

Broderick raised his eyebrows. "Police officers investigating murders don't have to explain their presence anywhere," he reminded Craven gently. "What's much more to the point is what are you doing here?" He regarded Craven with bland curiosity.

"I came to see Chris Reynolds," explained Craven.

Broderick's eyes swept round the room, taking in the scattered furniture. "So did I," he said. "Two minds with but a single thought. Where is Reynolds?"

"I don't know," said Craven. "He certainly isn't here."

"Obviously not," said Broderick. He indicated the shambles. "How did this happen?"

"Don't ask me," said Craven petulantly. "I've only just arrived."

"Had you an appointment with Reynolds?"

"No."

"What did you want to see him about?"

"I'm writing an article on his sister, and I want some information."

Broderick dropped his casual manner and his voice became authoritative. "How well did you know Billie Reynolds, Craven?"

"I didn't know her—not to speak to, at any rate."

"But you must have known her," persisted Broderick. "After all, as a journalist and local correspondent you must have made it your business to know everyone round here."

"Nevertheless, I didn't know her," said Craven with a show of spirit. "As a matter of fact, I only saw her twice. The first time was at a regatta, the second in a pub at Maidenhead."

"When was that?"

"About two weeks ago."

"Was she alone?"

"No, there was a man with her. A local chap—fellow I'd seen before."

"Really?" said Broderick curiously. "And who was it?"

Craven smiled enigmatically. "It was you, Sergeant," he said. . . .

The telephone was ringing insistently as Henderson hurried into his study. There was about him an air of suppressed excitement and he was breathing quickly. A bloodstained handkerchief had been wrapped hastily round his right hand. He crossed the room in two quick strides and picked up the receiver.

"Hallo, who's that?"

The voice at the other end said quietly: "This is Cooper." He sounded as unconcerned and unemotional as ever.

Henderson took a large, leather-covered book from his pocket and put it on the table. "It's all right, Cooper," he said, "I've got the diary. There's nothing to worry about."

"Good," said Cooper. "Now, listen. There's another slight complication. Maria Rocello's arrived and she's in Medlow."

"In *Medlow?*"

"Yes, she's staying at the White Hart."

"Well, what do you want me to do?"

There was a brief pause. "It's a little difficult," said Cooper at length. "I'm leaving for Liverpool tomorrow."

"You remember what you suggested?" said Henderson.

Cooper's voice sounded thoughtful. "Yes," he said slowly. Then more decisively: "All right, take care of her. You know exactly what to do?"

"Yes, I know," said Henderson. "Good night, Cooper." He hung up and stood for a moment, thinking. Then he picked up the diary and locked it in a drawer of his desk. He flipped quickly through the pages of the local telephone directory, picked up the receiver again and asked for the number of the White Hart Hotel. When they answered he said that he wanted to speak to Miss Maria Rocello. . . .

Maria Rocello thoughtfully replaced the receiver. Her conversation with Henderson had given her some food for thought. He had, she admitted to herself, a nice voice; cultured and entirely pleasing to the ear. She shrugged her shoulders in an unmistakably foreign gesture. Inspector Ford wished to be informed about anyone who contacted her.

"Yes?" said Ford's voice.

"Inspector," said Maria Rocello, "I've just had a call from that man you mentioned—David Henderson. He wants to see me."

"When?"

"Tonight."

"Where?"

"At his flat: he said any time after nine o'clock."

"What did you say?"

"I asked him why he wanted to see me and he said he'd like to talk to me about my brother. What should I do, Inspector?"

Ford's voice came over the wire to Maria incisively and firmly. He said: "Keep the appointment. Take a taxi and leave the hotel about nine o'clock."

"Very well," said Maria.

"One more thing," said Ford, "if Henderson offers you a drink on no account accept it. Good-bye, Miss Rocello."

Maria replaced the receiver thoughtfully.

In spite of his pleasant voice and easy manner, she wondered if there was something sinister about this David Henderson.

Henderson looked cheerful and alert as Maria Rocello came into the room. He was freshly shaved and had changed into a dark suit. Maria studied him warily and decided cautiously that, with certain reservations, she liked him. She noticed that there was a piece of sticking plaster on his right hand.

He came towards her with hand outstretched. "It's extremely nice of you to come, Miss Rocello." Clearly, he was endeavouring to put her at her ease. "I appreciate it very much."

Suddenly unsure of herself, Maria said: "You said over the telephone there was something you'd like to tell me about—my brother."

Henderson smiled. His teeth, Maria noticed, were very white and even. "There is indeed," he said. "Do sit down."

Maria sat on the chair he indicated and continued to watch Henderson covertly. He went on in the same casual tone: "You must have been a little surprised when you got my phone call."

"I was," she said. "I don't remember Paul—my brother—ever mentioning you, Mr. Henderson."

"I don't expect you do," said Henderson. He paused for a moment. "I was so sorry to hear about your brother. It was a dreadful shock to all of us."

"All of us?" said Maria curiously.

"Those who knew him," said Henderson.

"And how well did you know him, Mr. Henderson?"

"We met in Venice just after the war. I was in Italy for four years. Er—what part of Italy do you come from, Miss Rocello?"

"Florence."

"Ah, Florence!" said Henderson with enthusiasm. "What was it Shelley said about——"

"Mr. Henderson," broke in Maria, "how did you know I was in Medlow? How did you know I was staying at the White Hart?"

Henderson smiled, an enigmatic smile. Maria felt faintly irritated. For some reason that she could not properly define she had the feeling that Henderson was playing with her. Henderson turned towards the cupboard and opened it. Inside Maria could see a number of bottles and glasses.

"A man called Craven told me," said Henderson. "He's a journalist and knows all the local gossip."

"I wonder why Mr. Craven thought that I was a subject for gossip," said Maria coldly.

Henderson shrugged. "You know what these reporters are," he said easily. He had taken a decanter from the cupboard and was pouring a drink.

"Is that the man who wrote the article about my brother and Count Paragi—'The Murder of a Frogman'?"

Henderson nodded. "That's the chap. A curious young man, but quite talented in an odd sort of way." He turned and Maria saw that he had two full glasses in his hand. "Do have a glass of sherry, won't you?"

She said hesitantly: "No—no, thank you——"

"Nonsense!" said Henderson pleasantly. He handed her one of the glasses. "How long are you staying in Medlow?"

"That depends."

"On what?"

"On—a number of things."

There was a brief pause. Maria looked at the pale amber liquid in her glass and then put it down on a small table at her side.

Henderson broke the silence. "Miss Rocello," he said, "correct me if I'm mistaken. You came to England for two reasons. One: because you want to know why your brother was murdered."

"Is that so unnatural?"

"Not at all." Henderson held up the second finger of his right hand. "Two: because you want to know who murdered him."

Maria said: "You are not mistaken. Those are exactly the reasons why I came to England."

"Strange as it may seem," said Henderson, "I can answer both questions."

She said tensely: "You can?"

"Yes, I can." Henderson smiled at Maria, lifted his glass towards her and took a sip at his sherry. "But you're not drinking your sherry, Miss Rocello. It's very nice sherry—I really recommend it."

Maria looked at the glass on the small table. "Do you mind if I don't drink it?" she said apologetically. "I'm afraid I'm not very fond of sherry."

"I'm so sorry," said Henderson contritely. He moved towards the cupboard again. "Something else, perhaps? I have a bottle of Campari——"

"Nothing, thank you," said Maria adamantly.

"Quite sure?"

"Perfectly, thank you."

"Ah, well——" Henderson took another sip at his own drink. He said: "Did you speak to Inspector Ford after I telephoned you?"

Maria said: "Inspector Ford? Who is Inspector Ford?" Her voice sounded unconvincing, even to herself.

"He's the gentleman you saw this evening at six o'clock," said Henderson.

"I'm sorry, but I don't know what you are talking about," said Maria coolly. "I don't know anyone called Ford.

Henderson smiled gently and looked at Maria's untouched glass of sherry. He picked it up and held it critically up to the light. "It seems a pity to waste it," he remarked and drained it with every evidence of enjoyment. He looked at Maria quizzically. "You didn't think I was trying to poison you, did you?"

Maria gave a rather embarrassed little laugh. "No, no, of course not."

Henderson assumed a more serious expression. He said: "Miss Rocello, you may not believe it but I was a very good friend of your brother's. Because of that I'm going to give you a piece of advice. I hope you'll think it's good advice."

She said coldly: "Well?"

"I'm going to suggest that you return to Italy immediately."

"Why should I do that?"

"Because there's no reason for you to stay here."

"On the contrary," she said, "I consider that I have a very good reason for staying. I want to know why my brother was murdered, and who murdered him. When I find that out I will return to Italy, but not before."

"I see," said Henderson thoughtfully. He twiddled the stem of the glass he was holding. "And if I give you the answers to those two questions, will you return to Italy tomorrow morning?"

"Mr. Henderson," said Maria with disconcerting shrewdness, "if you know who murdered my brother, why don't you inform the police?"

Henderson did not answer the question. Instead, he said: "You're serious about staying here, in Medlow?"

She nodded. "Certainly I am. I told the inspector that——"

"Yes?" encouraged Henderson, "you told the inspector what?"

Furious with herself for being tricked into admitting that she had seen Ford, Maria compressed her lips and did not reply.

Henderson said casually: "Well, tell me what you told the inspector."

Maria's eyes flashed defiantly. "I told him that I had every intention of staying here until the case was solved or closed."

"I see," said Henderson quietly. He crossed the room to his desk and unlocked a drawer. He took out a photograph album and flipped through its pages. Then he took out a photograph and looked at it intently before passing it to Maria. "There are two people in this photograph," he said. "Tell me who they are." His voice was no longer casual; now it was brisk and efficient.

Slightly puzzled by Henderson's sudden change of manner, Maria studied the photograph. "One is my brother," she announced at once; "the other is my fiancé, Carlo Marissa."

"When was the photograph taken?"

"About two years ago."

"Where?"

"At Sorrento—outside the Hotel Excelsior."

"Who took it?" Henderson's interrogation was polite but inexorable.

"I did."

Henderson turned the photograph over and read the writing on the back. "Full marks, Miss Rocello," he said. "You're doing very well so far." He took a second photograph from the album and showed it to Maria.

"But where did you get these photographs from?" asked Maria, temporarily nonplussed. "This album is my brother's."

"Quite," said Henderson. "Now, this one. Who is this lady?"

"My aunt."

"And where was this taken?"

"In Rome, outside my aunt's villa."

"When?"

"About a year ago."

Henderson replaced the photographs and snapped the album shut. "Thank you," he said pleasantly.

Maria said quickly: "But what does this mean? What is the point of all this?"

Henderson said: "I had to make certain of something, Miss Rocello."

"Make certain of what?"

"Of your identity, Miss Rocello." Henderson crossed to the telephone and asked the operator for "Trunks". He stood with the receiver at his ear, drumming gently on the table with his fingers.

"Mr. Henderson," appealed Maria, "who are you? What was your connection with my brother?"

Henderson looked at her but did not answer. He said into the telephone: "I want a call to Liverpool, please—Hogarth 3701. A

114

personal call to James Cooper. This is Medlow 18."

"You haven't answered my question," said Maria levelly. "Who are you? Who is this Mr. Cooper you're telephoning?"

"James Cooper is a friend of mine," said Henderson. "Amongst many other attributes, he has a very persuasive tongue." He smiled briefly. "I think he'll persuade you to return to Italy, Miss Rocello. . . ."

Inspector Ford and Doctor Sheldon sat together in Ford's office. They were discussing the medical report on the death of Billie Reynolds.

"I still don't see," said Ford, tapping the foolscap report in front of him with the stem of his pipe, "how you can be so certain that death was caused by strangulation." He frowned. "Agreed, there were definite marks on the throat, but the body had been in the water a week, if not longer. Isn't it possible, therefore, that——"

"The marks were caused by someone taking the girl by the throat and throttling her," interrupted Sheldon some-what testily. "I can give you a lot of long words and high falutin' medical verbiage, but the plain fact of the matter is that——"

"She was strangled," put in Ford in a conciliatory voice.

"Exactly," said Sheldon patiently.

"Please don't think I'm trying to be difficult, Doctor," said Ford, "but my superior, Superintendent Harringay, didn't think your report was quite detailed enough."

Sheldon sighed. "I might have known," he said. "Your usual police surgeon was quite right. The last thing he said to me was: 'Remember, they won't be happy without a lot of fancy words, old boy.' " He smiled indulgently at Ford. "With all due respect to the senior ranks of the police force, they probably wouldn't know what a quarter of these long words mean. Come to that, I don't know what half of 'em mean myself."

Ford grinned back at Sheldon. "All right, Doctor," he said, "you win."

Sheldon said: "By the way, I don't know whether I ought to tell you this, but Henderson came to see me."

"When?" asked Ford quickly.

"Yesterday afternoon. He knew about Billie Reynolds's murder, and he wanted to know how it happened."

"How it happened?" said Ford.

"Yes, he wanted to know the cause of death."

"And did you tell him?"

"I merely told him she'd been murdered. I said if he wanted any further information about it, he'd better talk to you."

"Thank you," said Ford quietly.

"I said the right thing, did I?"

"You certainly did."

"It seemed to me that Henderson was pretty worked up about something," continued Sheldon. "It almost seemed as if——" He broke off hesitantly as Broderick came into the room.

"Yes, Doctor?" prompted Ford.

Sheldon shook his head. "I mustn't let my imagination run away with me," he said. He picked up his bag and prepared to leave. "It's just that—well, I've known Henderson for quite a long time now, and I like him. I have an idea that Katherine likes him too—which might make it a little difficult, to say the least."

"I don't quite see what you mean," said Ford.

"Don't you?" said Sheldon sadly. "I mean that if you arrest Henderson for the Rocello murder, Katherine's your principal witness."

"We haven't arrested him for anything yet," said Ford with a touch of severity.

"Er—no, of course not," said Sheldon apologetically. He looked from Ford to Broderick and back to Ford again. "Well, good-bye, Inspector. You know where to find me."

When Sheldon had gone Broderick said: "What's biting him? Why was he talking about Henderson?"

"Henderson went to see him," said Ford. "Apparently he was curious about the medical report." A puzzled frown wrinkled his forehead.

"I don't understand this, Bob. If Henderson was responsible for the murder, or even mixed up in it, he *must* have known how Billie Reynolds died."

"He probably did know," said Broderick cynically, "and was trying to pull the wool over our eyes."

"Hmm ... possibly ... well, did you see Miss Rocello?"

Broderick nodded. "Yes, I saw her. I've got some news for you too; she's flying back to Italy tomorrow morning."

Ford said, surprised: "Tomorrow morning?"

"That's right."

"But yesterday she was determined to stay here," said Ford. "Why, I even suggested that she should return, she——"

"Yesterday was yesterday," said Broderick. He sat himself on the arm of the chair facing the desk and lit a cigarette. "She's a different gal this morning."

"How d'you mean?"

"You saw her last night," said Broderick, "when she was tense and worried. Today she's quite different—not a care in the world. You wouldn't think it was the same girl."

Ford got up from his desk and stood looking at Broderick. "But why the sudden change?"

Broderick shrugged. "I wouldn't know."

"It's damned queer," said Ford thoughtfully. "Didn't she give you any sort of explanation? Didn't she say why she'd changed her mind?"

"Never gave a clue," said Broderick, with the indulgent air of a man who has an all-embracing understanding of women. He grinned suddenly and impudently. "But she paid you a very handsome compliment." He spread his hands in what he imagined to be a foreign gesture. "She said you impressed her ve-e-ery much."

Ford was still worried. "What the hell's all this about?" he demanded in exasperation. "This has happened since last night—since she saw Henderson."

Broderick's mood of flippancy had disappeared. "That's right," he said.

"What happened last night?"

"I've told you, Mike."

"Well, tell me again."

"She went to see Henderson as arranged," said Broderick. "She stayed at his place for about an hour. When she came out, we picked her up and drove her to the White Hart. She seemed a little excited, I thought, but sort of reticent—certainly quite different to what she was like earlier." Broderick leaned forward and stubbed his cigarette-end out in the ash-tray on Ford's desk. "I asked her how she got on, and she said that Henderson simply said that he was a friend of her brother's and if he could do anything to help her while she was in Medlow, he would. There you have it, Mike."

"How did Henderson know that she was in Medlow in the first place?"

"Apparently young Craven told him—at least that's what he told Miss Rocello. You know Craven, can't keep his long nose out of anyone's business."

Ford stroked his jaw. "Would you say she was sold on Henderson?" he asked.

"Completely," said Broderick with emphasis. "I thought so last night; this morning I'm certain of it."

"You reckon Henderson persuaded her to go back to Italy?"

"Yes, I do."

"I'd like another word with the girl," said Ford. "Don't let her leave Medlow without seeing me."

"I'll phone her," said Broderick.

P.C. Sanders came into the office carrying an envelope. "For you, sir," he said, handing it to Ford. "From Mr. Stacey Boyd."

Ford took a sheet of notepaper from the envelope. He read the letter and frowned.

"More trouble?" queried Broderick.

Ford looked up. "You remember that note Ralph Merson got with the earring?"

"Yes. The one in Henderson's handwriting."

Ford tapped the letter. "That's just it, Bob. Apparently it isn't in Henderson's writing."

"But it was," said Broderick. "Damn it, we checked it all ways. It was the same writing that we saw on Roger's exercise book and on the note that Craven received."

Ford shook his head. "No go, Bob," he said, "not according to old Stacey Boyd and he's the expert. He says the Craven note and the correction in the exercise book are in Henderson's writing. But the note to Merson is a copy—a good copy, mind you—but nevertheless a copy, of the same handwriting."

"But it can't be," said Broderick incredulously. "He must have made a mistake."

"Well, if he's mistaken about this, he could be mistaken about the others," said Ford. He looked at the letter again and then flicked the middle finger of his right hand on it. "But somehow I don't think he is. . . ."

With a quickness born of long experience, Robin Craven placed one foot inside the door of Maria Rocello's hotel room as soon as she opened the door. She eyed the slightly shabby figure somewhat dubiously. Surely, it was not customary for young men to force their way into bedrooms of English hotels. But Mr. Craven was not in the least disconcerted.

"I am sorry to disturb you, Miss Rocello," he apologized smoothly. "I'm a reporter—Robin Craven's the name—local correspondent of the *Daily News*. Do you think you could spare me a few minutes?"

Rather unwillingly, Maria admitted him.

"Now, what is it you want?"

Craven switched on his charm.

"You're thinking: 'Who is this confounded intruder? Why doesn't he mind his own business?' Isn't that it?"

"I wasn't thinking about you at all," said Maria with an indifference that she did not entirely feel. "I asked you what you wanted."

Craven spread his hands in an expressive gesture. "Of course, if you're busy I'll call back later." He produced a disarming smile. "Honestly, I have your interests *very* much at heart."

Maria relented a little. "If you've got any questions to ask," she said, "you'd better ask them now."

Craven's smile was full of self-satisfaction. He said: "Miss Rocello, you only arrived in Medlow yesterday and yet you're flying back to Italy tomorrow morning. Why?"

"I'm sorry, but I do not understand you?"

Graven smiled doggedly. "But why such a quick visit? Have you already accomplished what you came for?"

Maria looked at Craven suspiciously. "How do you know that I'm returning tomorrow morning?"

"You've reserved a seat on the 10.30 plane from London Airport," said Craven with careless patronage.

"You appear to be well informed, Mr. Craven," said Maria frigidly.

Craven preened himself. "Well, I do *try*," he said modestly. "But I'm not *quite* so well informed as I'd like to be." He started to pace gently backwards and forwards. "I wrote an article about your brother, you know."

"Yes, I know. I read it."

"In that article I said that your brother was a great friend of Count Paragi."

"Well?"

"Yesterday morning," continued Craven in measured tones, "*The Globe*"—he spoke of *The Globe* as he would of a socially inferior cousin—"chose to contradict that statement for some obscure reason. They said that your brother and Count Paragi were just wartime acquaintances. They quoted a recent statement, apparently made by Paragi himself, to that effect."

"So?" said Maria.

"So I'd like to get the point clear," said Craven amiably. "Am I right or the illustrious *Globe?* Was your brother a friend of Count Paragi's or wasn't he?" He regarded Maria with quizzical benevolence.

"Either way I cannot see that it's of great importance," said Maria indifferently.

"Oh, but you're wrong," said Craven fervently, "it's extremely important. The person who murdered your brother had a motive. In common with a number of other people I'd like to know what that motive was."

"Would it help you if you knew whether Count Paragi was a friend of my brother's or not?" asked Maria.

Craven deliberated this question for a moment. Then he said slowly: "Yes, I think it might."

Maria said: "I'm afraid I can't answer your question."

This time Craven's smile was not without malice. "Can't or won't?" he inquired.

"I can't," said Maria simply, "because I do not know the answer. My brother had his own circle of friends. Whether Count Paragi was one of them, I do not know."

"Did you ever meet Paragi?"

"Once," said Maria, "about a year ago,"

"Where?"

"In Genoa."

That's a bit better, thought Craven, the answers are coming a bit more readily now. He had always prided himself on his polite and persuasive methods of questioning. He decided to embark upon a really thorough interrogation; and was on the point of framing his next question when the telephone rang. "Did your brother introduce you to him?" he asked as Maria turned and picked up the telephone.

"I can't remember who introduced me," said Maria with a trace of irritation. "And now, if you'll excuse me——"

Broderick's voice came over the line, cheerful and confident. He said: "This is Sergeant Broderick. Inspector Ford would like to see you before you leave. Do you think you could drop in sometime this evening?"

Maria hesitated. "I'm catching the 6.40 train to London," she said, "and I don't want——"

"That's perfectly all right, Miss Rocello," interrupted Broderick. "Be here at six o'clock and I'll run you to the station. You'll catch the train all right."

"Yes, all right, Sergeant," said Maria, "and thank you."

Broderick sounded pleased. He said: "Thank*you*, Miss Rocello."

Craven returned to the attack. "We were talking about Count Paragi," he reminded Maria. "You were just going to tell me who introduced you to him."

"I don't remember who introduced him," said Maria tartly. "It was at a cocktail party. I'm sorry, Mr. Craven, but there's nothing else I can tell you."

"But you haven't answered my question," protested Craven, gently chiding, infinitely patient. "Why are you returning home so soon?"

Maria realized that there was no point in losing her temper with Robin Craven. True to type, he would continue his tireless and thick-skinned probing until he had his story tailored and pre-digested to the last syllable.

"I wanted to make sure that your police were making every effort to find my brother's murderer," she said with somewhat unsettling candour.

Craven took the remark in his stride. "And are you quite satisfied now?"

"Yes, perfectly. I've seen Inspector Ford and . . . I'm quite satisfied."

Craven made a little gesture. "What a pity you didn't telephone me. I could have saved you a journey."

"What do you mean?"

Craven shrugged expressively. "I could have told you," he said with superb condescension, "that our police are wonderful."

Katherine Walters was putting the finishing touches to a dress design. She worked quickly and skilfully with a drawing-board on her knee. Every few minutes she cocked her head to one side to survey her efforts. It could, she reflected, become one of the best drawings she had ever done, if only she could give her full concentration to it. But her thoughts continually strayed to the murder of Paul Rocello, to Inspector Ford and—somewhat unwillingly but none the less persistently—to David Henderson. She felt vaguely annoyed with herself for thinking about Henderson; outwardly he was good-looking, charming and kind. But the fact remained that he was still under the gravest possible suspicion in connection with the murders of Paul Rocello and Billie Reynolds, and seemed to be going to considerable pains to obstruct the course of justice. She shook her head vigorously as if to rid herself of thoughts about anything save fashion designing, picked up her pencil again and concentrated once more on her drawing-board.

Doctor Sheldon came into the room with the weary air of a man who has done a hard and unrewarding day's work. He left his medical bag on a table and said: "Hallo, Katherine."

"Hallo," said Katherine. "You sound a bit weary. Had a hard day?"

"Somewhat," said Sheldon and stifled a yawn.

"I'm afraid you haven't quite finished yet," she said sympathetically. "Mr. Hobson's in the consulting room."

"I know," said Sheldon. "Judy told me." He stared at Katherine's drawing. "What's that supposed to be?"

"What does it look like?"

"Looks like a coat of some sort."

Katherine laughed. "It is a coat," she said. "That's the first drawing of mine you've recognized. One of us is improving. What about a cup of tea?"

"Nothing I'd like more," said Sheldon with longing, "but I suppose I'd better see old Hobson first—he might be really ill for once."

"You never know," said Katherine, "although he looked as well as ever."

Sheldon sighed again. "I've had quite a day, Katherine. I've had nearly two hours with Ford. I'll be mighty glad when Jennings gets back."

"What did Ford have to say?"

"Very little." Sheldon frowned slightly. "I find Ford a very difficult man to weigh up."

"Does he still suspect David Henderson?" Katherine's voice sounded apprehensive, even to herself.

"Yes, I think so," said Sheldon after a moment's thought, "but he seems reluctant to commit himself. By the way, they say Rocello's sister's in Medlow and that she saw Henderson last night."

"Who told you that?"

"I overheard Ford talking to Sergeant Broderick."

Katherine said: "I saw something in the paper this morning about a man called Harringay from Scotland Yard."

"Ah, yes," said Sheldon.

"But I thought Ford was in charge of the case?"

"So he is, but he's answerable to Harringay." Sheldon made a grimace. "It was Harringay that complained about my report—the silly fool didn't think it was detailed enough. Obviously I was never meant to be a police surgeon." He looked at his watch and sighed. "Well, I suppose I'd better take a look at old Hobson. I expect he's coughing as well as ever."

"No, his cough's better," said Katherine.

"Is it?"

"Oh, yes. Quite recovered, he says."

"Well, what is it this time?"

"He's got sciatica."

Sheldon heaved another sigh, picked up his bag, and went off to the consulting room, his shoulders drooping with weariness.

Sheldon had barely left the room when Judy came in. She said: "Mr. Craven would like to see you, miss, if you can spare him a few minutes."

"Ask him to come in, please, Judy," Katherine said. She placed her drawing-board by the side of the settee, out of sight.

"How *nice* to see you, Miss Walters," said Craven effusively.

Katherine said shortly: "If you want to see my uncle he's——"

"But it's you I want to see," interrupted Craven.

"Oh," said Katherine without enthusiasm.

"I just wanted to ask your advice about something."

"My advice?"

"Well, I suppose you wouldn't call it advice really," said Craven obscurely. "It's just that I'd like you to do a little thing for me—if you can, that is."

"What is it you want me to do?"

Craven said: "I believe you speak Italian, don't you?"

"Yes, I do," said Katherine. "Why?"

Craven smiled conspiratorially. "Ah, then it shouldn't be difficult."

"What shouldn't?" She was finding it increasingly difficult to be polite.

Like a conjuror producing a rabbit from a hat Craven took a single piece of blotting paper from his inside pocket. He said: "There's something written on this piece of blotting paper in Italian.

I'd be grateful if you'd translate it for me."

Katherine looked at the blotting paper in bewilderment. "You'll have to hold it up to a mirror," Craven explained.

Katherine looked at Craven sharply. Then, her curiosity getting the better of her, she crossed to a mirror hanging on the wall.

"Well?" said Craven, "what does it say?"

"It says," said Katherine, reading slowly, " 'He's been very kind to me, and I consider it—er—a stroke of luck that I came here. I feel infinitely happier than I ever expected.' I think that's right so far."

"Jolly good," said Craven. He had been writing busily as Katherine read out the letter. "Any more?"

"It goes on," continued Katherine, " 'I'll explain why when . . . I see you.' That's all." She turned and faced Craven. "Who wrote this? Why did you ask me to translate it for you?"

"It was written by a friend of mine," said Craven glibly, "and he lost the original." Katherine's face registered stony disbelief. "It's most kind of you to take so much trouble," continued Craven. "I'm really very grateful. Give your uncle my kind regards."

He gave her another ingratiating smile as he hastily pocketed his notebook. In fact, he seemed so anxious to be gone that Katherine at once suspected that the message she had translated was in some way connected with a news story.

She stood at the window and watched him walk rapidly down the road. At the corner, he went straight into the telephone box without looking round.

Maria Rocello was in her room at the White Hart at Medlow, packing preparatory to leaving for Italy. She paused, a folded dress half-way into her suitcase, as someone knocked at the door.

"Come in!" called Maria. She placed the dress in the case and turned to see Katherine Walters.

"Miss Rocello?" inquired Katherine.

"Ye-e-es," said Maria slowly.

"I'm so sorry to disturb you like this," said Katherine, "but I wonder if you could spare me a few minutes? I'd very much like to have a word with you."

Maria closed the suitcase. She said cautiously: "Who are you? Are you a newspaper reporter? Because if you are——"

"I'm not a reporter," reassured Katherine. "My name is Katherine Walters. I'm staying in Medlow with my uncle, Doctor Sheldon."

"Please don't think me rude," said Maria, "but I have an appointment at six o'clock."

"What I've got to say won't take very long," said Katherine. Maria paused uncertainly. "I think it's in your interest that you should see me, Miss Rocello," Katherine continued pointedly, "as well as mine."

"Very well, Miss Walters," said Maria.

"Miss Rocello," said Katherine, "I'm going to ask you a rather strange question, but I've a very good reason for asking it. Did you write a letter this morning?"

"Why, yes, I did," said Maria.

"Who was the letter to?"

"To my fiancé," said Maria. "He's in Paris and I wrote to say—" she broke off in sudden annoyance—"what business is it of yours whether I wrote a letter or not?"

Katherine said: "A man called Robin Craven came to see me this afternoon. He knew I spoke Italian, so he asked me to translate something for him."

"Well?" said Maria, puzzled; "What has this got to do with me?"

"The words he asked me to translate," said Katherine slowly, "were on a piece of blotting paper. I have a feeling it was taken from your desk." She looked in the direction of a small writing bureau which stood in the corner of the room.

Maria quickly crossed over to the bureau and examined the blotting pad. She saw that part of the blotting paper had been torn away.

"What was on the blotting paper?" asked Maria tensely.

"Don't worry," said Katherine. "Mr. Craven wasn't quite as clever as he thought he was—or so lucky. It simply said, 'He's been terribly kind to me, and I consider it a stroke of luck that I came here. I feel much happier than I did. I'll explain why when I see you."

Maria was visibly relieved. "Is that all it said?"

"That's all," said Katherine.

Maria inclined her head graciously. "Thank you for telling me."

Katherine said earnestly: "Please don't think me terribly inquisitive, but who were you referring to when you said 'he's been terribly kind to me'?"

"I was referring to someone I've met since I've been down here," replied Maria.

"Was it David Henderson?" hazarded Katherine.

"What do you know about David Henderson?" countered Maria defensively.

"I know that at any moment he's likely to be arrested," said Katherine, "and I shall be a witness—the principal witness, in fact."

"What do you mean?"

"I mean that I saw Henderson the afternoon your brother was murdered," said Katherine. "I saw him leave the houseboat."

"David Henderson?"

Katherine nodded. "Yes."

"You must be mistaken," said Maria incredulously.

"I wish I were," said Katherine, "but I'm not."

A faint smile hovered about Maria's mouth for a moment and she looked searchingly at Katherine. She said: "I met David Henderson last night for the first time. Somehow, I don't think he murdered my brother."

"Was it Henderson you referred to in your letter?" asked Katherine.

"Yes," said Maria. The faintly enigmatic smile still fingered on her lips. "May I ask *you* a question, Miss Walters—it's rather a personal question?"

"Well?"

Maria enunciated each word with care. "Are you in love with him?"

Katherine laughed, not without a hint of embarrassment. "Good Heavens, no! Why, I've only seen him twice."

Miss Rocello said: "And what has that got to do with it?"

Chapter Eleven

Detective-Inspector Michael Ford sat at his desk writing a report. From time to time he paused to refresh himself from a cup of tea at his elbow.

The wrinkled frown of concentration suggested that the writing of long and detailed reports did not come easily to Ford. The fountain pen in his large hand seemed curiously puny and inept. Nevertheless, his handwriting was incongruously small and neat: his phraseology a model of clarity.

He was hunting in his mind for a suitable phrase when he was interrupted by the simultaneous ringing of the telephone and Broderick's appearance.

"Miss Rocello's here," announced Broderick.

Ford reached for the receiver. "All right, I'll see her in a minute. Hallo?"

A strong, cheerful voice said: "Is that Detective-Inspector Ford?"

"Speaking," said Ford.

"*The* Detective-Inspector Ford?"

"Yes," said Ford irritably. "What is it you want?"

The voice laughed. "You haven't lost your bark, Inspector. Still as fierce as ever!"

Ford scowled at the receiver. This joker on the other end had certainly picked the wrong moment for being funny.

"Who the devil is that?" he demanded.

"Just a voice from the past," said the voice. "It's Harry Vincent."

Ford's scowl instantly vanished and his face split into a delighted grin, "Harry Vincent!" he said in amazement. "Well I'll be.... Harry, where the devil are you speaking from?"

"I'm in a call box at Henley," said Vincent, "on my way up North. I reckon we ought to have dinner together, for old times' sake."

"Bet your life, Harry," said Ford enthusiastically.

"I'll pick you up at the office in about half an hour."

"Fine," said Ford. A sudden thought struck him. "Oh, by the way ... how's the old ticker?"

"Much about the same. Still misses a beat when it feels like it. See you in about half an hour."

Ford was still grinning as he put the receiver down. "That was Harry Vincent," he told Broderick. "D'you ever meet him?"

Broderick shook his head. "Often heard you talk about him, but I never met him."

"Wonderful scout, old Harry," said Ford. "We used to be great friends in the old days."

"He retired, didn't he?" said Broderick.

"That's right. Damn shame, really, he was just coming up for promotion to Chief Inspector."

"What happened?"

"Heart went dicky on him. Had to pack up."

"What's he doing now?"

"Damned if I know," said Ford. "Someone told me he had a job with some firm or other." He stacked his papers neatly on the desk. "I'd better see Miss Rocello now, Bob."

Broderick poked his head through the adjoining door. "Please come in, Miss Rocello," he said.

Maria came into the office and regarded Ford and Broderick with complete equanimity. Ford went straight to the point. He said: "Sergeant Broderick tells me that you're returning to Italy almost immediately."

Maria nodded. "That is correct, Inspector. You see, I am taking your advice."

"You didn't seem very keen on taking my advice yesterday afternoon," said Ford. "You said that you intended to stay here until the case was solved."

"I know that," said Maria easily. "I changed my mind."

"Why?" asked Ford bluntly.

Maria shrugged. "Women do, you know," she said disarmingly.

"I am aware of that," said Ford dryly. "All the same, I'd like to know what caused you to change your mind about leaving."

"I've thought the matter over," said Maria casually, "and I've come to the conclusion that there's nothing I can do here. There is no possible reason for me to stay."

Ford leaned forward in his chair. "This decision has been taken since you saw David Henderson," he said.

Maria nodded. "That is true," she admitted, "but it is not as a result of my interview with Mr. Henderson."

"I find that difficult to believe," said Ford.

"I am sorry about that, Inspector," said Maria with complete composure, "but it happens to be true." She rose to her feet in a quick, graceful movement. "I'm afraid I must be going now." She smiled at Ford as she left the office.

The inspector glared across at Broderick and brought his fist down on the desk with a resounding bang. "Why don't you do something, ladykiller?" he said bitterly.

"Who is it this time?" wondered Mrs. Williams as she went to answer the front door bell. There had been a strange assortment of visitors for Mr. Henderson since the murder inquiry. Some of them made her feel very uncomfortable; they were not the types a gentleman like Mr. Henderson had usually entertained.

She opened the front door to a correctly dressed middle-aged man who seemed rather nervous. He spoke politely enough and looked as if he might be a member of a respectable profession. At least, that was something.

"There's a Mr. Merson to see you, sir," Mrs. Williams told Henderson.

"Ah, yes, Mrs. Williams," said Henderson. "Show him in, will you?"

Merson came into the room quickly. He was palpably ill at ease. He waited until Mrs. Williams had closed the door before favouring Henderson with a baleful and suspicious look.

"Mr. Merson?" said Henderson, getting up.

"Yes," said Merson aggressively.

"I'm David Henderson. It's so good of you to call. Do sit down, won't you?"

"I'd rather stand," said Merson malevolently. He flourished a piece of paper at Henderson. "Perhaps you'd be good enough to tell me what's the meaning of this note."

"I should have thought it was fairly obvious," said Henderson gently. "It means I'd like to talk to you."

"Talk to me about what?"

"About a lady called Reynolds—Miss Billie Reynolds." Henderson was watching Merson closely.

Merson started visibly but quickly recovered himself. "I don't know anyone called Reynolds," he said.

"No?" said Henderson. He smiled at Merson. "You must have a very short memory. On Thursday, July 5th you took Miss Reynolds to London. On Friday, August 3rd you went down to Brighton and met her at the Grand Central Hotel. You stayed there together until Tuesday, August 7th."

Merson was biting his lower lip in some agitation. A nervous tic distorted his left cheek and betrayed his uneasiness. His hands gripping the back of a chair showed the whites of the knuckles.

"You seem remarkably well informed," he said in a tone edged with sarcasm.

"I make a point of it," retorted Henderson coolly.

Merson was losing his control rapidly.

"Suppose you come to the point," he snapped. "What the hell's all this about?"

"I shouldn't lose your temper with me, Mr. Merson," said Henderson in a gently chiding voice. Then it became firm and authoritative. He snapped: "I want something from you, Mr. Merson, and I want it now."

"What do you want from me?" Merson's voice had lost much of its truculence.

"Information," said Henderson.

"About what?"

"Firstly," said Henderson in calmly judicial tones, "what did Miss Reynolds call you? Did she use your Christian name or had she a nickname for you?"

Merson bridled. "What the hell business is it of yours what Billie Reynolds called me?"

"I'm asking you a question, Mr. Merson," said Henderson. No one could have doubted that he expected an immediate and true answer. "It may seem a strange question, but I assure you that it's a very important one. What did Miss Reynolds call you?"

Merson said sulkily: "If you must know, she called me Dandy." He brought up his chin with a jerk and fixed Henderson with hostile eyes. "And if you want to know *why* she called me Dandy——"

Henderson held up a hand. "I don't," he said calmly. "You've answered my question, and I'm satisfied."

All fire seemed to have gone out of Ralph Merson. He sat down on the arm of the settee. He said quietly: "You knew the answer, didn't you?"

"I knew that Miss Reynolds was friendly with someone she called Dandy," said Henderson, "but I wasn't sure who it was. Now I am."

"All right, so it was me," said Merson. He sounded tired and deflated. "Have you any other questions you'd like to ask?"

"Yes, I have," said Henderson. He crossed over to the desk and picked up the diary. "You see this?"

"Yes. What is it?"

"It's a diary," said Henderson. "It belonged to Billie Reynolds."

Merson stared at the diary as if mesmerized. He said, "Billie's! My God——"

"There's a lot of interesting information in this diary, Mr. Merson," went on Henderson amiably, "including several references to a gentleman called 'R'."

"You mean the letter 'R'?"

Henderson nodded. "That's right." He opened the diary and flipped through the pages. "Ah, here we are . . . ' "R" came to see me soon after it was dark. I wish I didn't feel this way about him.

I just don't know whether to trust him or not.' " Henderson looked at Merson keenly. "Do you know who she was referring to?"

"I've no idea," said Merson. His attempt to appear casual was a signal failure.

Henderson continued relentlessly: "Did she ever mention anyone to you whose name—presumably Christian name—began with the letter 'R'?"

Merson shook his head. "I can't think of anyone."

"You're sure?"

"Of course I'm sure," said Merson irritably. He ceaselessly moistened his lips with his tongue. He said tensely: "Where did you get that diary?"

"I got it from a gentleman called Chris Reynolds," said Henderson. "He was a little—er—reluctant to part with it, but he did."

"And what are you going to do with it?" asked Merson apprehensively.

"I'm going to keep it," replied Henderson. He added: "For the time being." He sat back in his chair and regarded Merson with complete equanimity.

Merson said: "Look, Henderson, let's be perfectly frank with each other."

"By all means," murmured Henderson.

"I'm mentioned in that diary," went on Merson. "I must be."

"You are," agreed Henderson. "You are indeed."

Merson said grimly: "I'll give you two thousand pounds for it."

Henderson raised his eyebrows. "Two thousand pounds?" he said. He shook his head reprovingly. "Come, come, Mr. Merson. I should have thought it was worth much more than that. . . ."

Ford advanced across the room with hand outstretched. "Well, Harry," he said warmly. "By heaven, it's good to see you."

Harry Vincent, or to give him his proper title, ex-Detective-Inspector Harry Vincent, was about fifty years of age. He was of medium height and inclined to plumpness—a plumpness that was deceptive, for Vincent had scarcely an ounce of superfluous flesh on him. He was totally unlike the popular conception of a plain-clothes policeman; he could have been a bank manager, an insurance salesman or a commercial traveller. He was the type of man that goes unnoticed in crowds, which in his particular profession was just as well.

The two men shook hands. "It's been a long time, Mike," said Vincent, "too damn' long."

"You're looking well, Harry," observed Ford. "Don't look as if you had a care in the world."

"I wouldn't go so far as to say that," said Vincent. "You look pretty good yourself, Mike. How's Roger?"

"He's fine. He's at Rockingham College, you know—got a scholarship."

"Yes, I heard about that. Gets his brains from his old man, no doubt."

"No doubt," agreed Ford. "But let's hear about you, Harry. What have you been doing with yourself lately? What's it like to be retired?"

Vincent did not answer the question immediately. He said: "You seem to be in the news these days, Mike."

"Suppose I am," said Ford wryly. "We've got quite a case on our hands, you know. But let's skip the shop; what have *you* been up to?"

"I've been abroad for six months," said Vincent.

"Lucky chap," commented Ford. "On holiday?"

"Ostensibly," said Vincent evasively.

"How's the heart now, Harry? Still troubling you?"

"It never did trouble me," was the surprising reply. Vincent patted his chest with every indication of confidence. "It's always been pretty good."

"But I thought you retired because of a weak heart."

"That's what people were meant to think," said Vincent casually. Ford stared at him in bewilderment. Vincent went on: "As a matter of fact, Mike, I came up from London specially to see you."

"To see me?" said Ford.

"That's right. I'm on my way up North."

"I see," said Ford slowly. He looked at Vincent shrewdly. "What's all this about, Harry? Anything the matter?"

"There's nothing the matter," said Vincent in the same casual voice, "except that you're in for one or two surprises."

"After the last couple of weeks nothing's going to surprise me much," returned Ford. "What sort of surprises do you mean?"

"I'll put you out of your misery, Mike," said Vincent. "To start with, I never did have a weak heart, and I didn't retire."

"Didn't retire?" said Ford in amazement, "but you *did*. Damnit, we had a dinner! I made a speech!"

"I'm not likely to forget that," said Vincent.

"We gave you a silver salver," pursued Ford. "It was smothered in ruddy signatures."

"I know," said Vincent regretfully. "I've always felt a bit guilty about that salver."

"Now look, Harry," said Ford, "what exactly is all this about? Are you serious?"

Vincent nodded. "Perfectly," he said.

"But if you didn't retire," said Ford in near exasperation, "what the hell *did* you do?"

"I was put in charge of a new department."

"Where? At Scotland Yard?"

"Well, not exactly at the Yard, Mike," said Vincent. "I'm working with Sir Edward Westerby."

"Sir Edward Westerby!" Ford could not conceal a note of awed respect. He did not know a great deal about Westerby's activities for the very good reason that Sir Edward went to considerable pains to keep them secret; Ford knew, however, that he controlled a world-wide organization with seemingly unlimited Treasury funds for the purpose of keeping a jump ahead of those alert cosmopolitan entrepreneurs who were quite unscrupulous in exploiting international crises for their own private profit. Ford was obviously impressed.

"So you're in Intelligence, eh Harry?"

Vincent smiled. "You've got it at last, Mike."

Ford rubbed his chin thoughtfully. "That's right outside my beat," he said.

"Don't be so sure, Mike. I'm here to put you in the picture, as the politicians say."

Ford said: "What d'you mean—in the picture?"

Vincent smiled. "Rocello isn't dead, you know."

Ford said: "Not *dead?* What the hell d'you mean?"

"Exactly what I say. He's not dead."

"You mean Paul Rocello, the Italian who was murdered?"

Vincent nodded. "That's the man, except that he wasn't murdered."

"But of course he was murdered!" said Ford. "I saw the body."

"You saw *a* body, Mike. It wasn't Rocello's."

Ford clutched his desk with both hands. "Are you sure? Do you know what you're saying?"

"I'm saying that Rocello isn't dead," said Vincent calmly.

"Then where is he, for God's sake?"

"He's in Canada." Vincent looked at his watch; "or he will be within the next four or five hours."

Ford slapped his forehead with the palm of his hand. "Am I going mad?" he demanded. "I tell you, I saw——"

"Just a minute, Mike," said Vincent soothingly. "There's a chap outside I'd like you to meet."

"Oh?" said Ford, "who's that?"

"He's a colleague of mine," said Vincent. He smiled. "We call him The Other Man."

"Give me strength," said a bewildered Detective-Inspector Ford.

Vincent opened the door and beckoned outside. "You can come in now," he said.

Ford sat bolt upright in his chair and stared open-mouthed at David Henderson. . . .

"Hallo, Inspector," said Henderson, "how are you. . .?"

It took Ford a full minute to recover the power of speech. He said: "Henderson . . . but what——?"

Henderson turned to Vincent. "Have you told him?" he asked.

"I've told him about Rocello," said Vincent, "but that's all."

"I think you ought to tell him the rest of the story," said Henderson. He smiled at Inspector Ford. "My appearance seems to have given Inspector Ford a bit of a shock."

"It has," said Ford grimly. "It's been quite a day for shocks, one way and another."

"I really must apologize for all the trouble I've caused you," said Henderson. "My turning up now must have been the last straw."

Ford sighed. "Well, at least I know you didn't murder Rocello," he said, "because he's not dead."

"I didn't murder anyone, Inspector," said Henderson. "But there's a certain gentleman I'd gladly murder if I could get my hands on him."

"There have been quite enough murders already," said Ford. A semblance of a smile belied the grimness of his voice and he turned appealingly to Vincent. "Don't you think you'd better tell me the rest of the story? After all, I am the police officer in charge of the case." He looked at Henderson with a wealth of meaning, but the smile still hovered round his lips. "One or two people have made the solution of this murder a little difficult, to say the least."

"I know, Inspector, I know," said Henderson. "Believe me, I'd have made it easier if I could."

"I'll tell the tale," said Vincent. "If I don't, I've a shrewd suspicion that Henderson will. . . ."

Vincent settled himself more comfortably in his chair.

"It all began," said Vincent, "in 1941. Does the name *Kirbydale* mean anything to you, Mike?"

"Can't say it does," said Ford.

"The *Kirbydale*," went on Vincent, "was the name of a naval tanker. On the 10th September, 1941, she was lying at anchor in Gibraltar Harbour. It was a lovely, hot day—the sort of day you could almost forget there was a war on. Suddenly, to everyone's amazement, she was blown sky-high. One minute there was ten thousand tons of good, solid shipping—the next, absolutely nothing. Two Italians were responsible for that little job"—Vincent paused for a moment—"Count Paragi and Paul Rocello. Believe me, Mike, they made a *really* thorough job of blowing up the tanker."

Ford said: "Go on, Harry."

"At that early period of the war," continued Vincent, "no one knew a lot about underwater warfare—it was very much in the pioneer stage. Paragi and Rocello were two of the pioneers. They did a lot towards developing the limpet bomb and the launching of the first human torpedo. Well, we know the sort of things those boys got up to in the war. Now, over fifteen years later, the thing has been brought to a fine level of perfection." Vincent broke off to light a cigarette. He went on: "When the war was over Rocello continued to be very interested in naval warfare." He turned to Ford. "Now, here's the really interesting part. He became very friendly with Henderson who, unknown to Rocello, was attached to Intelligence."

Ford looked at Henderson. "I've often wondered just what you were up to during the war, Mr. Henderson," he said. "Now I'm beginning to get the idea. Go on, Harry."

"I was working for Naval Intelligence myself at the time," continued Vincent, "and Henderson sent me a report. He said that Rocello had started work on a new project, an apparatus to combat Briggs D."

"Briggs D?" said Ford, mystified.

"Briggs D," explained Vincent, "was an explosive which was used for underwater vibration work. The effect of this——"

"Wait a minute, Harry," complained Ford, "don't get too technical. I don't even know how my 'fridge works. I'm only a simple copper, remember."

Henderson laughed. "I'll put it in ordinary language for you, Inspector."

"I'm not all that dim," said Ford, "but all this underwater stuff's got me a bit foxed." He looked apologetically from Henderson to Vincent. "What is this Briggs D effort exactly?"

"Briggs D," explained Henderson, "was a special kind of depth charge used by ships for detecting frogmen or human torpedoes."

"I see," said Ford.

Henderson went on: "This device produced a series of underwater convulsions, vibrations if you like, and everything—literally everything underwater, within a certain radius, was killed instantly."

"I'm beginning to get the idea," said Ford. "Rocello was working on an apparatus which would defeat Briggs D., something that a frogman would wear as a sort of antidote. Is that it?"

"Exactly," said Henderson. He turned to Vincent. "Supposing you go on from there."

Vincent took up the tale. He said: "This work of Rocello's went on for some years. About six months ago, however, one of our agents—a man called Cooper——"

"Cooper!" said Ford. "I was wondering how he fitted into this business."

"You'll find out in a minute," said Vincent. "Cooper—and you can take it from me, Mike, he's a pretty tough handful—reported that certain other people were interested in Rocello's experiments—people who could do a whole lot of damage. It was then that we decided to bring Henderson into the picture.

"It seemed likely that Rocello might be in very considerable danger," supplied Henderson. "So I went to Italy and persuaded him that it might be a lot safer to continue his experiments over here."

"Rocello wasn't completely safe even in England," continued Vincent. "So—he had to die."

"I see," said Ford. He grinned ruefully. "You people certainly do things the hard way, don't you?"

"It was the only way, Mike," said Vincent. "The only thing to do was to give the impression that Rocello had been murdered. We did just that."

"How?" asked Ford.

"You should know, Mike," said Vincent slyly, "that you can always find a dead body in England if you want one badly enough. Well, we got one and we planted it on the houseboat—as Paul Rocello, deceased."

"I always thought you were wasted in the police force, Harry," murmured Ford admiringly. "But what about this anonymous note young Craven got?"

"Henderson sent that note," said Vincent.

"We badly needed publicity," explained Henderson, "all the

publicity we could get. We had to convince everyone that the dead man *was* Rocello."

"We knew that Craven would get excited about the frogman story," said Vincent, "and give us all the publicity we needed."

"You certainly know how to pick 'em, Harry," said Ford. "Craven's been one of the biggest headaches I've had on this case—and that's saying something."

"He was a natural," agreed Henderson.

Ford said: "I'm beginning to see a bit of daylight now. The night that Billie Reynolds saw you——"

"We were planting the body," supplied Henderson. "Rocello had already left for Liverpool."

"But that was in the early hours of the morning," protested Ford. "Katherine Walters saw you the following afternoon."

"That's right," said Henderson.

"But you'd already planted the body by then. Why go back to the houseboat?"

"There was a bit of a slip-up," explained Vincent. "Cooper, who was in charge of the whole operation, forgot Rocello's wrist watch. It was flown down from Liverpool and Henderson went back to the houseboat with it."

"I see," said Ford. He looked at Henderson. "What about Billie Reynolds? How does she come into all this?"

"We were a bit worried about Billie," confessed Vincent. "She'd seen far too much for our liking. So we took her away from Medlow and put her in a flat in Chelsea."

"The hell you did," said Ford.

Vincent smiled reminiscently. "Billie was a bit of a handful so we had to slip her a Mickey Finn. When she came to she was livid and had a nasty hangover on top of it."

"We couldn't explain the true position to her," said Henderson, "so we had to make up a story—I flatter myself it was quite a good one. Unfortunately Billie didn't do as she was told. She gave us the slip, came back to Medlow and contacted a friend of hers."

"And it was this 'friend' who murdered her?" said Ford.

"Yes," said Vincent quietly. "We're quite sure of that."

"Well, who is he?" asked Ford.

"He's a local man," said Vincent. "We've had our eye on him for some little time."

"What's his name?"

Vincent looked across at Henderson. Henderson took Billie Reynolds's diary out of his pocket and handed it to Ford.

"Billie refers to him in her diary as 'R'," said Henderson.

Ford, who had been thumbing through the diary, looked up. " 'R'?"

"Yes," said Henderson, "there are a number of references to him, but she never gave him a name."

"Is this 'R' a foreign agent?" asked Ford.

"He's an agent, all right," said Vincent. "He was put in specially to watch Rocello."

"And he's a local man?"

"Yes."

"Have you any idea who he is?"

"We've a pretty good idea," said Vincent. "The trouble is catching the gentleman."

"We've damn well got to catch him," said Ford grimly. "The fact that he's a foreign agent is your department. But he's a murderer as well, and that is strictly *my* pidgin."

"I know that, Mike," said Vincent seriously. "We've all got to pull together on this. . . ."

Chapter Twelve

"I've got Doctor Sheldon on the line for you, sir," said the telephone operator at Police Headquarters.

"Thank you," said Ford. "Hallo—that you, Doctor?"

"What can I do for you, Inspector?" asked Sheldon.

"I've had another memo through about the Reynolds report," said Ford. "I wonder if you'd mind dropping in to see me sometime this afternoon."

"Four o'clock suit you?"

"Fine," said Ford. "I'll look forward to seeing you then."

Ford replaced the receiver and finished the letter he was writing. He put the letter in an envelope, stuck it down and addressed it. He then pressed his bell.

"See that this is delivered to Mr. Vincent," instructed Ford, handing the letter to a uniformed constable. "The address is on the envelope. There's no need to wait for a reply."

The constable left the office as Sergeant Broderick came in.

"Something happened, Mike?"

Ford said: "Quite a lot's happened. I've got some news for you about the Rocello case."

"Yes?" said Broderick.

"First of all," said Ford, "don't waste any more time on Henderson."

Broderick was clearly puzzled. "What d'you mean?"

"Just what I say," said Ford. He was busy locking some of the drawers in his desk. "I mean Henderson's out—he's no longer a suspect."

Broderick registered complete amazement. "But Mike," he

exploded, "he's our *principal* suspect! If we cross Henderson off our list, where the hell are we?"

"I thought that might shake you a bit, Bob," said Ford.

"But it's crazy," protested Broderick. "It means we're right back where we started. Damn it, we could pull Henderson in any time——"

"Listen to me, Bob." There was a rasp of authority in Ford's voice and Borderick fell silent. "You've got to accept what I say without question. Henderson is definitely and positively *out*. He's produced an alibi."

"He needs a ruddy good one," said Broderick unbelievingly.

"He's got a perfect one," said Ford.

Broderick scratched his head in utter mystification. "But if he's got an alibi why the hell hasn't he produced it before? What——"

"No more questions, Bob," said Ford. "Forget about Henderson. He's off the list. Got it?"

Broderick shook his head sadly. "O.K.," he said resignedly, "you're the boss. But don't expect me to believe that story."

"What d'you mean?" asked Ford sharply.

"I just think it's rather odd that Henderson should take so long producing this alibi," said Broderick. He shrugged his shoulders expressively. "I don't pretend to understand this. Maybe it's none of my business, but——"

"But what?" said Ford.

"Look, Mike," said Broderick, "you surely don't believe all this stuff about Henderson's alibi—it's just a bit too good to be true. Something else has happened, something much bigger than just a murder."

Ford smiled in an avuncular way at Broderick and patted him on the shoulder. "Let's leave it like that, shall we?"

Broderick said: "All right, so Henderson's off the list. But where do we go from here?"

Ford went over to his desk, opened a drawer and took out Billie Reynolds's diary. He said: "The late lamented Billie Reynolds kept a diary. She made several references to a man she called 'R'. 'R' is the man we're after—he's the man who killed her."

"Are you sure of this?" asked Broderick.

"Absolutely positive."

" 'R'," said Broderick thoughtfully. He fingered his chin for a moment and then suddenly looked up. "Ralph——"

"Thinking of Ralph Merson?" said Ford.

"Yes. Aren't you?"

Ford shook his head. "No go, Bob. Billie had a nickname for him." He patted the diary. "She uses the nickname all the time in here."

"What did she call him?"

"Dandy."

"Blimey," said Broderick. He added: "I know what I'd call him ... Mike, can I look at the diary a minute?"

Ford handed the diary to Broderick, who slowly turned the pages.

"What are you looking for?" asked Ford.

"I'm looking to see if she was ill at any time."

Ford said: "You're thinking of Sheldon."

"Well, it's a possible idea," said Broderick.

"As you say, it's an idea," said Ford slowly. "Doctor *Richard* Sheldon. . . ."

Henderson stood at the window of his study, looking out on to the quadrangle of Rockingham College. His hands were thrust deep in his pockets, a cold pipe clenched between his teeth. Vincent sat, pensive and relaxed, in an armchair.

Henderson turned to face Vincent. "I still think it would be a lot safer to use one of your own people instead of young Craven."

"I don't agree," said Vincent. "If Craven's caught there's an outside chance they'll think he's just a snooper—the local newshound trying to dig up a bit of news for his paper."

"Contrary to general belief, journalists don't usually break into other people's houses," said Henderson.

"I know that," said Vincent. "But supposing I did use one of my own men and 'R' recognized him?"

"That would be tricky, I admit," said Henderson.

" 'R' would be out of the country before we could say 'knife'," went on Vincent. "Using Craven we've got nothing to lose, providing he keeps his head."

"How did he react to the suggestion?" asked Henderson.

Vincent smiled. "He was a bit shaken at first, but he'll do it all right. I asked him to call round and have another talk about it."

"By the way," said Henderson. "Did you get the handkerchief you wanted?"

"They're sending one down from London," said Vincent. "Incidentally, I've had a note from Ford. He's arranged to see Sheldon this afternoon at four o'clock."

"Good," said Henderson. "I'll phone Katherine Walters later and make sure she's going to be in."

"That seems all right," said Vincent, "but what are you going to tell her when you see her?"

Henderson hesitated. "Well," he said uncertainly, "what we arranged to tell her—what you suggested."

"I know all that," said Vincent, "but what else?"

"I don't quite understand," said Henderson. "What d'you mean 'what else'?"

"Wouldn't you like to tell her the whole story as far as you're concerned?"

"Obviously I would," said Henderson,"but I can't without your permission."

Vincent said slowly: "My permission rather depends."

"On what?"

Vincent strolled towards the window and looked down on the quadrangle. This must be Henderson's real life, he thought. He sighed gently. You got hold of a man—a rather exceptional man—and you turned him into a first-class operative. But you never knew whether the man you had chosen was happy in his work. Indeed, one never asked. In the case of Henderson the time had clearly come.

Vincent waved a hand over Rockingham College. "Are you happy down here, Henderson?" he asked.

"Extremely happy," said Henderson, "and I want to stay that way."

Vincent gestured again towards the quadrangle outside and the school buildings on the other side. "All this," he said thoughtfully, "this is what you really want more than anything?"

"Yes," said Henderson simply.

Vincent turned and faced Henderson directly. "You didn't feel like that ten years ago," he said. "You said you'd do anything—anywhere—at any time."

"Who told you that?"

"Sir Edward Westerby," said Vincent.

"I saw the letter you wrote him."

"Ah, that letter," said Henderson. "But I didn't write it, you know. It was written by the Other Man, the man I told you about. The square peg in the round hole."

"And now you're a square peg in a square hole, is that it?"

Henderson nodded. "That's it."

Vincent said: "Sir Edward asked me to find out if you'd be interested in joining my department. I'd very much like to have you."

"No, Vincent," said Henderson, "you don't want me. You might want the Other Man, but he's dead." Henderson joined Vincent at the window and looked at the buildings of Rockingham College with something akin to love. "You see," he went on, "I buried that other man the day I came to Medlow. Anyway, I'm too soft for your department. The only time I get tough is when I administer six of the best to adolescent backsides and I doubt if even that hurts them very much."

" 'This is going to hurt you more than it hurts me'," quoted Vincent. "I wonder."

"I'm a schoolmaster and nothing else," said Henderson. "As far as your business is concerned I'm merely an amateur tucked away in his little backwater."

"I had an old lady working for me once," said Vincent inconsequently. "She was a leading light in the Women's Institute."

"Good for her," said Henderson. He smiled suddenly. "But at the moment I'm still working for you. What do I do next?"

"First of all," said Vincent, "you must tell your girl friend the whole story."

Henderson raised his eyebrows. "My girl friend?"

"Katherine Walters," said Vincent without subtlety. "Tell her everything, but keep me out of it."

"All right," said Henderson, "but do you mind if I point out one small mistake you've made?"

"Not at all," said Vincent, "in my peculiar trade one frequently learns by mistakes."

"Katherine Walters is not my girl friend," said Henderson in measured tones.

"Just as you say," murmured Vincent. "Tell her the whole story just the same. Better lose no time about it."

"I'll see to it right away."

As Henderson walked towards the door Vincent stood watching him.

". . . So, you see," said Henderson, "if Cooper hadn't forgotten the wrist watch, there wouldn't have been any necessity for me to go back to the houseboat and you wouldn't have seen me." He smiled wryly. "I can't tell you how anxious I've been to clear myself in your eyes."

Katherine said simply: "I'm glad." They sat in silence for a moment. It seemed suddenly almost as if they were meeting for the first time without a dark cloud of suspicion hanging between them. Gradually they were becoming aware of one another and they both liked what they saw.

"But why didn't you tell me all this at the time?" asked Katherine. "I'd never have gone to the police." She did not add that it was only after much mental wrestling that she had come to such a decision. "But—well, you must admit, it did *look* suspicious."

"It could hardly have looked more so," agreed Henderson. "But I couldn't tell you because I was sworn to secrecy." He looked at her very frankly and she suddenly knew a feeling of unaccountably violent relief. They were two people talking normally together; talking without innuendoes, excuses and deception.

"In any case," pursued Henderson, "if I'd told you about the watch, you'd have guessed that the dead man wasn't Rocello."

"Where is Rocello now?" asked Katherine.

"He's in Canada."

"And is his work—what you were telling me about—completed?"

"As far as we're concerned, yes," said Henderson. "You see, the first part of his work—the most important and far-reaching experiments—could only take place in Europe; that's why we had to be sure that he wasn't being watched—why we wanted certain people to think he'd been murdered."

"I'm beginning to understand," said Katherine thoughtfully. She leaned forward in her chair. "Mr. Henderson, you remember the evening you came to see my uncle about your shoulder?"

"Yes."

"It was me you really wanted to see, wasn't it?"

"Indeed it was," said Henderson. He looked at her quizzically. "Did you mind?"

Katherine blushed momentarily. "I'm being serious," she said.

"So am I," said Henderson. "Please go on."

"Why did you want to see me so specially?"

Henderson said: "We knew that there was an agent in the district watching Rocello, and we thought perhaps——"

"You suspected *me?*"

"We couldn't be absolutely sure about anyone. Quite honestly, we didn't know who to suspect." Henderson smiled. "After all, you *had* just come back from the continent; you *were* on the river; you *could* have been watching the houseboat. We had to be sure."

"Of course," said Katherine. "In fact, I was half asleep in the sunshine and trying to read an extraordinarily dull book."

"Well, we don't suspect you any more," said Henderson. "Otherwise I wouldn't have invited myself to tea."

"I'm glad you did," said Katherine.

With the milk jug poised over Henderson's cup, Katherine said: "May I ask you a very personal question?"

"Please do."

"Are you really a schoolmaster or—are you in Intelligence?"

Henderson sipped his tea appreciatively. "I'm a schoolmaster at Rockingham College and I've every intention of remaining one."

"Then how on earth did you get mixed up in all this?"

"I was attached to Naval Intelligence during the latter part of the war," explained Henderson. "That's when I first met Paul Rocello. When this business blew up, they asked me to take a hand in it because I knew a little about what Rocello was trying to do."

"Was it as important as all that?"

"All the top brass thought so," said Henderson seriously.

Katherine said: "I suppose now that this business is all over——"

"It's very far from being all over, I'm afraid," interrupted Henderson. "I told you just now that there was a foreign agent in Medlow, watching Rocello."

"Yes?"

"Well, he's still here."

"But how d'you know?"

"Because we know who it is."

"You know?"

"Yes," said Henderson quietly, "we know."

Katherine said: "Then this is the man that murdered Billie Reynolds?"

Henderson nodded. "That's right. And I want to talk to you about him; that's why I'm here."

With gradually widening eyes, Katherine Walters listened to David Henderson. . . .

The hands of the clock on Henderson's mantelpiece pointed to a quarter to three. Henderson yawned and stubbed out a cigarette. The overflowing ash-tray and the dryness of his mouth told their own story.

Vincent had lost a little of his characteristic imperturbability. Every few minutes he got up from his chair to look through the curtains. He compared his watch with Henderson's clock.

"Something must have happened to Craven," said Vincent uneasily. "He should have been here an hour ago."

"Supposing we drive round to the house and see," suggested Henderson.

"We'll give him another fifteen minutes," decided Vincent. "If he's not here by three o'clock we'll do that."

On a tray at Henderson's elbow stood a bottle of whisky and a soda syphon. "What about a drink?" said Henderson.

"Good idea," said Vincent. Henderson poured out two generous measures and splashed in a little soda. Vincent said: "He left here just after twelve. How long would it take him to get there?"

"About twenty minutes," said Henderson.

"Say he got there at half-past," said Vincent, "then half an hour to get the lie of the land. Fifteen minutes to——"

"Just a minute," interrupted Henderson, "I think I heard a car." He moved quickly to the window and looked through the curtains. Below him he could see two headlights. "That's him."

"Good," said Vincent, swallowing his drink. "He had me worried for a moment. . . ."

A few minutes later when Robin Craven entered he was far from being his usual self. He wore a shabby black macintosh, a battered trilby, gloves and rubber-soled shoes. A blood-stained handkerchief was wrapped round his left hand; in his right he carried a document case. He looked pale, drawn and exhausted.

Henderson said: "What happened? You've been a hell of a long time."

"My God, I should think so!" said Craven. "The car dried up on the way back and I had to walk a mile for petrol." A glimpse of the old Robin Craven flashed forth. "If there's one thing I *loathe* more than another it's walking."

Vincent looked at his bandaged hand. "You've cut yourself," he said.

"Just a scratch," said Craven indifferently, "but it wouldn't stop bleeding."

"Well, what happened?" asked Vincent.

Craven shed his macintosh and threw it onto a chair. He flung the trilby after it, smoothed back his hair and said: "Breaking into the house was easy—no trouble at all. Everything went like

150

clockwork, just as we planned it. I think I'd make a pretty useful burglar."

"Go on," said Vincent.

"I was in one of the bedrooms," continued Craven, "having a good look round when I heard footsteps outside." He paused dramatically. "Possibly housebreaking is not my métier after all. I've never been so petrified."

"What happened?" asked Vincent.

"By the time he'd opened the door and switched the light on I was behind a wardrobe. I thought he was never going. Believe it or not, I was behind that damn wardrobe for almost an hour."

"It's a good job he didn't see you," said Vincent grimly.

"It's a wonder he didn't hear my teeth chattering," retorted Craven. He picked up the document case and handed it to Vincent. "I can't tell you how thankful I am to be rid of this."

Vincent smiled briefly and opened it. He began to examine the letters and photographs inside.

"What about the handkerchief?" asked Henderson.

"That's all right," said Craven. "That was the first thing I did." He nodded towards the document case. "That was in a cupboard"—he added with a touch of pride: "I had to force it open. Incidently, there was a radio there as well—a short-wave set."

Vincent smiled broadly and clapped a hand on Craven's shoulder. "You did very well, son," he said. "I'll see you don't lose by it."

Henderson said to Vincent: "Did you get what you wanted?"

Vincent nodded significantly. "Yes," he said, "I got just what I wanted."

"I think we might have a drink," said Henderson. "Craven certainly looks as though he could do with one."

"I certainly could," said Craven feelingly.

"Whisky?"

"Yes, please."

Vincent looked up from a letter he was reading. "Give him a large one," he said, "he's earned it."

"It could hardly," said Robin Craven, "be *too* large. . . ."

Chapter Thirteen

Police Constable Sanders was a comfortably built man who always welcomed a spell of station duty at Headquarters. It should not be supposed that he was lazy, but at the age of forty-seven he considered himself entitled to reasonably comfortable working conditions. He had spent the greater part of a quarter of a century out of doors in all weathers and both his feet and his chest had suffered in consequence. Promotion to sergeant at his age was out of the question, but Sanders would not have welcomed more responsibility than he had at present—a wife and four children were enough for any man. Station duty at Medlow would suit him until he fell due for his pension.

Sanders was not averse to a little outdoor work when there was a football match or a local regatta. But on the whole he enjoyed the even tenor of life at Headquarters where the telephone, the lost property book and the inquiries desk were the essential adjuncts to his working day. Of course, these two murders added a certain spice to life as long as he was not expected to wade about in the river up to his waist or lurk about on street corners half the night.

P.C. Sanders took a surreptitious look at the racing page of the daily paper which reposed invitingly next to a pile of routine correspondence—there was little doubt in Sanders's mind which should have priority of his attention . . . Red Monk looked to have been thrown in at a handy weight and should, with reasonable luck, start at a decent price. It might even be worth doubling him with Spartan King in the last race.

Sanders was interrupted in the solution of this vexatious problem by the appearance of Ralph Merson, and Merson was clearly not in the best of tempers.

"I want to see Inspector Ford at once," he announced without any preamble.

"Sorry, sir," said Sanders, "I'm afraid the inspector's very busy. He can't see anyone at the moment."

"But I've got to see him. It's very important."

"Sorry, sir," said Sanders again. "But those were my instructions from the inspector."

"I'm not the slightest bit interested in your instructions, Constable," said Merson glacially. "I demand to see Inspector Ford at once."

Sanders emitted a gentle sigh. Men like Ralph Merson had long since ceased to perturb him. He had known many such men in his long service: if you pinched 'em for a parking offence it seemed that butter wouldn't melt in their mouths. It was only when they thought they were in the right that they started shouting the odds.

"The inspector can't be disturbed at the moment, sir," said Sanders soothingly but with infinite finality.

Merson's nose twitched as if scenting impertinence. "What d'you mean, he can't be disturbed? Who the hell does he think he is, the Prime Minister?"

"Sorry, sir," said Sanders with all-embracing patience, "Inspector's orders."

"Now, look here, Constable," said Merson threateningly, "I wouldn't recommend your present attitude. I want to see Inspector Ford at once, understand?"

"Yes, sir," said Sanders. He thought: I'd like to shove you in a cell, you frosty-faced basket. Without losing any dignity he said: "I'll see if Inspector Ford is free, sir."

"I should damn' well think so," said Merson. He eyed the retreating figure of P.C. Sanders with extreme malevolence.

Ford was writing busily and looked at Sanders with some irritation. "Well, what is it?"

"Sorry, sir," said Sanders, "but there's a gentleman to see you. I told him you didn't want to be disturbed but——"

"But he got nasty, did he, Sanders?" said Ford sympathetically. He remembered occasions when he had been a constable on station duty. "Who is he?"

"His name's Ralph Merson, sir," said Sanders. "He's in a proper state about something."

"Merson, eh?" said Ford. "All right, Sanders, ask him to come in."

"Very good, sir," said Sanders. He stalked towards the door and there was fierce disapproval in every step.

"Oh, and Sanders?"

Sanders turned. "Sir?"

"Put me a dollar on Red Monk, will you?"

Sanders grinned. "Leave it to me."

"The inspector will see you now, sir," he said to Merson. Ralph Merson brushed past him with purposeful disregard.

"Good morning, Mr. Merson," said Ford amiably.

"I've been waiting in that confounded office since nine o'clock," said Merson.

"I'm sorry, Mr. Merson," said Ford. He leaned back in his chair and regarded Merson with extreme benevolence. "What can I do for you, sir?"

Merson leaned both hands on Ford's desk. He said gratingly: "Did you break into my house last night?"

Ford just perceptibly raised his eyebrows and indicated a chair. "Won't you sit down, Mr. Merson?"

Merson glowered, but sat in the proffered chair. He said: "Well?"

"Now, Mr. Merson, you were saying——?"

"I asked," said Merson in a more controlled voice, "if you or one of your men broke into my house last night. I should like an answer."

Ford smiled indulgently. "Part of the duties of the police is to *prevent* people from breaking into houses."

"Well, someone broke into mine last night," said Merson.

"I'm sorry to hear that," said Ford, "but what makes you think I had anything to do with it?"

Merson swallowed. He said: "Look here, Ford, I'm going to be very frank with you."

"By all means, Mr. Merson," returned Ford equably. "I must say you're doing very well as it is."

Merson leaned across the desk. "You think *I* murdered Billie Reynolds, so you had my house searched last night."

"But why should we search your house, Mr. Merson?"

"Because you were looking for something."

"What, for instance?"

"Billie was strangled with something," said Merson on the same note of aggression. "A rope or a piece of cord, perhaps."

"And you think that's what we were looking for?"

"Well, it's feasible, isn't it?"

"When did you discover that your house had been broken into?" asked Ford.

"This morning, at about seven o'clock. I saw the broken glass near the french windows."

Ford looked at Merson keenly. "Then why didn't you phone us straightaway?"

"Because nothing seemed to be missing," said Merson. His voice had lost some of its initial bluster. "I didn't want my wife to hear," he ended lamely.

"Well, I didn't break into your house, Mr. Merson," said Ford gently, "nor did I instruct anyone else to do so." He smiled reassuringly. "We do our best to give the taxpayer value for money, you know."

"Oh," said Merson doubtfully.

"If you ask me, Mr. Merson," said Ford, "you've been reading too many detective novels and not very good ones either." He got up from his chair as Broderick came into the office. To Broderick he said: "Someone broke into Mr. Merson's house last night. Take Morgan and see if there are any fingerprints. The usual routine."

"When did this happen?" asked Broderick.

"I'm not sure," said Merson meekly. "It must have been sometime during the night."

"A full investigation will be made," Ford promised Merson. He nodded to Broderick. "All right, Sergeant. Let me know how you get on."

Broderick said: "Yes, sir," and then went out of the office.

Ford turned to Merson again. "I hope, Mr. Merson," he said with a trace of irony, "that you consider that police action is being carried out with sufficient promptness." He could not resist a final dig. "If policemen *did* go round breaking into houses, then I think the taxpayer would have a legitimate grievance." He nodded courteously. "Good morning, Mr. Merson. . . ."

A few minutes later Broderick came back. "I didn't want to say anything in front of Merson," he said, "but we've had a report on Chris Reynolds."

"Well, what about him?" asked Ford.

"Apparently he's back in London: working for a greengrocer in the Edgware Road."

"Right," said Ford. "Find out exactly how he spent the last twenty-four hours. Get in touch with the Yard if necessary."

Broderick looked puzzled.

"Have *you* heard anything yourself about Chris Reynolds? There was nothing much in that report."

Ford said quietly: "Just check on the last twenty-four hours, Sergeant."

P.C. Sanders was tidying Ford's office preparatory to going off duty when Broderick hurried in.

"Where's the inspector?" asked Broderick.

"Don't know, Sergeant," said Sanders. "He went out just after four and I haven't seen him since."

"Any idea where he went?"

"No."

"D'you know whether he's coming back this evening?"

"I should think he is," said Sanders. "His son phoned about five minutes ago."

"Roger phoned up?"

"Yes," said Sanders. "He's not feeling too good—got pains in his tummy or something. Blimey, these kids are all the same. Now, take my eldest daughter. She'll get a headache when there's a bit of housework to be done but mention the pictures——"

Sanders's domestic anecdote was lost as Ford came in. He said tersely: "What's this in aid of? A committee meeting?"

"No," said Broderick apologetically, "I just wanted to——"

He was interrupted by Ford. "Has Superintendent Harringay phoned?" he asked Sanders.

"No, sir."

"Roger rang up," said Broderick, "says he's not feeling well."

"When was this?" demanded Ford.

"About five minutes ago, sir," said Sanders. "Said he'd got pains in his stomach and was going to bed."

"All right, Sanders," said Ford a trifle wearily, "you can shove off now." To Broderick he said: "That's all I needed! I've had a hell of a day and now Rosier has to fall ill."

"You look as if you could do with a drink, Mike," said Broderick sympathetically.

"By God, I could," said Ford feelingly. He looked at his watch. "Not much chance of having one, though."

"Why not?" said Broderick, "they open at six."

"I know," said Ford, "but I'm supposed to be seeing Miss Walters at six."

"Well, I'll see Miss Walters for you," suggested Broderick. "You nip home—take a look at Roger and have a couple of stiff ones. If it's anything important I'll ring you."

"Thanks, Bob," said Ford, "I'll be at home."

"What does she want to see you about?" queried Broderick.

"No idea," said Ford. "She simply rang and asked if I'd come round."

"Did she sound worried at all?"

"No, not that I noticed."

"Well, whatever it is, I'll sort it out," said Broderick cheerfully. "I hope the boy's all right."

"Oh, I don't expect it's anything very serious," said Ford, "but it's damn' funny how this always happens in the holidays. During term time he's always as right as rain."

"Too many ice creams and too much television, I expect," said Broderick, without much sympathy.

"I shouldn't be surprised," said Ford. He hunched his shoulders, and for the first time it occurred to Broderick that Ford looked a tired man. "Oh, by the way, how did you get on at Merson's place?"

"Well, to be honest, I can't quite figure that job out," said Broderick thoughtfully. "There's a pane of glass out of the french windows and it certainly looks as if somebody broke in, but—I don't know."

"How d'you mean 'you don't know'?"

"There just seems something a bit phoney about the whole thing, that's all."

"Any fingerprints?"

"Not a trace."

"Did anyone hear anything?"

"There was only Merson and his wife there. Neither of 'em heard a thing."

"What about Chris Reynolds? Did you check on him?"

"Yes, he's in London. He hasn't been down here for days."

Ford nodded, turned towards the door, and then stopped. "Did you see Mrs. Merson?"

"Yes, I saw her."

"What's she like?"

Broderick seemed to be at a loss for words. He tugged at the lobe of his right ear. "Well," he said at length, "she's certainly quite different from Billie Reynolds. If you saw her you wouldn't blame old Merson for going off the rails."

Ford laughed. "Just as I thought," he said and yawned. "Well, I'm off now, Bob. Give me a ring if anything turns up. . . ."

Chapter Fourteen

Judy, Doctor Sheldon's maid, poked her head round the door of the drawing-room. Katherine sat there alone, reading the evening paper. Judy said in a stage whisper: "Sergeant Broderick to see you, miss."

Katherine looked up. It was Judy's night off and it was obvious that, so far as outward appearances were concerned, she was leaving nothing to chance. She said: "Ask him to come in, will you, Judy?"

Broderick's entrance was characteristically breezy. He eyed Judy appreciatively before addressing Katherine. "Good evening, Miss Walters," he said.

Katherine said: "Good evening, Sergeant." Judy still hovered at the doorway. "It's your night off, isn't it, Judy?"

"Yes, miss," said Judy. Fred, the current boy friend, was of punctual habits and if she didn't get a move on she'd be late.

"Got your key?" inquired Katherine.

"Oh, yes, miss," said Judy, patting her handbag. Her eyes lingered on Broderick for a moment and in a moment of guilty disloyalty she compared him favourably with Fred. She suddenly realized that she was three minutes late already. "Good night, miss," she said hastily and left the room.

"Won't you sit down, Sergeant?" invited Katherine.

"Thank you, miss," said Broderick. He sat down on the edge of an armchair.

"Wouldn't you like to take your coat off?" asked Katherine.

"I won't keep you very long, Miss Walters," said Broderick. "Inspector Ford asked me to call round. He said you telephoned him this afternoon."

"That's right," said Katherine, "I did." She looked inquiringly at Broderick. "Isn't the inspector coming?"

"I'm afraid he couldn't manage it," explained Broderick. "That's why I'm here."

Katherine said: "I see. . . ."

"His son's been taken ill."

"I'm sorry," said Katherine, "I do hope it isn't serious."

"I doubt it," said Broderick. "Er—what exactly is it that we can do for you, Miss Walters?"

A tiny frown puckered Katherine's forehead. She said hesitantly: "I really think I ought to speak to Inspector Ford about this, Sergeant—it *is* rather important."

Broderick indicated the telephone. "I can send for him if you like, miss. . . ."

Katherine hesitated and bit her lower Up. "Well——"

"Perhaps if you gave me some idea of what it's all about . . ." suggested Broderick.

Katherine glanced quickly towards the door leading into the hall. She said: "It's about my uncle."

Broderick was obviously puzzled. "You mean Doctor Sheldon?"

"Yes."

"Well, what about Doctor Sheldon?"

Katherine said hesitantly: "I've found out something about him. It's—something that the inspector—the police—ought to know about."

Broderick said: "Go on, Miss Walters." His voice was concerned.

"I don't quite know how to tell you this," went on Katherine, "but two days before Billie Reynolds disappeared my uncle——" Katherine stopped talking as they both heard the front door open and close. She looked quickly towards the hall and then at Broderick. Broderick leaned forward in his chair. . . .

Doctor Sheldon's entry took them both by surprise. He was wearing his hat and overcoat and carrying his medical bag in his right hand. Clutched in his left hand was a small document case. He looked worried and out of breath and had clearly been running.

Katherine said: "Uncle . . . what's happened?"

Sheldon did not immediately answer, but crossed the room to the telephone.

"What's the matter, Doctor?" asked Broderick.

Sheldon was dialling a number. Over his shoulder he said: "There's been a car accident at Medlow Bridge—a fearful mess. Both drivers are very badly hurt." He tapped the receiver impatiently. "Katherine, there's a hypodermic in my cabinet. Fetch it for me, will you?"

As Katherine ran from the room, Broderick crossed over to Sheldon. "What happened exactly?" he asked.

"God knows," said Sheldon, "I've never seen a crash like it. A car hit one of those gravel lorries from Henley quarry." He broke off to tap the receiver again. "What the hell's the matter with this thing?"

"Do you know who was in the car?" asked Broderick.

"A chap called Berson or some such name," said Sheldon, "he's in a pretty bad way."

Broderick said quickly: "Was it Merson? Ralph Merson?"

"That's it," said Sheldon. "This blasted telephone——"

Katherine hurried in with a box in her hand. "I think this is it," she said.

Sheldon nodded. "Good girl," he said. He handed the telephone to Broderick and stuffed the hypodermic box into his bag. He said to Broderick: "Get St. Peter's Hospital—it's Medlow 22—extension 4. Tell 'em what's happened and say it's very urgent."

Broderick nodded and started tapping the receiver. He said loudly and impatiently: "Operator! God damn the thing . . . operator!"

Sheldon hastily picked up his medical bag and thrust the document case into Katherine's hand. He said: "This must have been thrown out of the car somehow. It belongs to the driver. Take care of it until I get back." He hurried out of the room.

Broderick eventually abandoned his efforts to get a reply on the telephone. He replaced the receiver and turned to Katherine. "There's something the matter with this phone—it must be out of order."

"It was perfectly all right this afternoon," said Katherine. "Are you sure there's no reply?"

Broderick tapped the receiver again. He said: "Dead as a doornail.

It's out of order, all right. I think I'd better go and find a box. If anything—" He was walking towards the door as he spoke and suddenly stopped dead. He stared at Katherine with narrowing eyes.

Katherine was opening the document case that Sheldon had given to her. She took out a photograph and several envelopes. She opened one of the envelopes and extracted a letter.

Broderick said softly: "Where did you get that letter from?"

Katherine looked up. She said: "It was in this case." She looked at the envelope again and then at Broderick. "It's addressed to you and it's from Billie Reynolds. It says: 'Dear Robert,'—that's you isn't it?—'I'm staying in London but I must see you——' "

"Give me that letter!" said Broderick. He came across the room with a kind of sliding shuffle; his fists were half clenched. Katherine hardly recognized the self-assured police officer that she had been speaking to a few minutes earlier. Broderick's mouth was closed in a thin, hard line. His features seemed, in some extraordinary way, to have changed slightly. Instinctively Katherine backed away from him. Then she stopped and faced him. She said: "There's a photograph of you here—with Billie Reynolds."

Broderick said: "I know. Those things were taken from my house last night. They belong to me." He held out his hand. "Give them to me, Miss Walters, please."

Katherine backed away so that there was a chair between Broderick and herself. "Why should Miss Reynolds want to meet you?" she asked in a voice that she scarcely recognized as her own. "Was she a friend of yours?"

Broderick came a little nearer. "That's none of your business," he said. "The letters and the photograph, please."

Katherine glanced at some of the other envelopes. Her heart beat faster as she saw some of the addresses. She said, trying to keep a growing tremor out of her voice: "You appear to have quite a few friends on the Continent, Mr. Broderick. Rumania—Czechoslovakia—Poland——"

Broderick suddenly sprang forward and viciously kicked over the chair that stood between them. "Give—me—those—letters!" He stood, in the middle of the room, his fingers crooked.

Katherine said: "These are for Inspector Ford and no one else."

Broderick moved towards her. Trying to anticipate his next move, Katherine felt like a mouse that finds itself confronted with a large and predatory tom-cat.

Broderick's voice took on a soft and indescribably menacing timbre. He said: "Miss Walters, I'm warning you. If you don't do what I tell you I'll——"

Katherine said: "You'll what, Mr. Broderick?"

Broderick did not answer but moved even closer.

Katherine said steadily: "You killed Billie Reynolds, didn't you?"

Broderick said: "I want those letters."

"You killed Billie Reynolds, didn't you?" repeated Katherine tensely.

Broderick lost the last remnant of his self-control. "Yes, I did!" he blazed. "I killed the little bitch! She started asking questions—all sorts of questions. She bloody well asked for it."

Katherine stared at Broderick with dilated eyes. He had taken off the blue scarf that he had been wearing. He advanced towards her slowly and inexorably, twining the scarf in his fingers.

"Now, Miss Walters," he said. His voice was soft and persuasive again, "Please don't be stupid about this. No one's seen those letters or the photograph, except you and Merson. Surely, the intelligent thing would be to——"

He was still coming towards her, with one hand outstretched for the letters. Katherine was gripping the table with both hands, as if to control her fear. When he was almost in reach of her, she suddenly made a supreme effort and lifted the heavy table until it tilted on two legs, then crashed towards him so that he had to leap quickly to avoid it. With a couple of rapid strides she was at the door that led into the hall and had flicked off the light switch:

Realizing that it was only a matter of seconds before he found the switch, Katherine moved swiftly towards the window and hid behind the heavy curtains. She could hear him blundering into the furniture and cursing in a voice that sounded even more frightening in the dark. There was a click and the lights went on.

Broderick stood by the door looking round the room. He knew

she must still be there, for he would have heard a door open if she had escaped that way. He noticed a key on the inside of the door leading to the hall, and carefully turned it. Then he crossed towards the consulting room and stood for a moment undecided. He had just made sure that Katherine was not hiding behind the settee when a movement of the curtains caught his eye. He stood quite still for a couple of seconds, then reached out and tore savagely at the curtains.

The man standing there with arms akimbo was so motionless that he might have been an image.

"Henderson!" gasped Broderick. "What the devil are you doing here?"

Henderson stared at him for a few moments without replying, then let his arms fall to his sides. Broderick recoiled a pace.

"As you seem to be under some misapprehension, Sergeant, I thought I might explain one or two things. . . ."

"Such as?"

"In the first place, you seem to have the idea that the photograph and those letters have only been seen by Ralph Merson and Miss Walters. They've been seen by quite a number of people as a matter of fact, though Merson doesn't happen to be one of them."

"Don't be a damn fool!" said Broderick, who appeared to have recovered some of his nerve. "Merson took them from my room last night."

Henderson shook his head.

"I can understand your getting that impression, but you're wrong, Sergeant. Right off the beam. You broke into Merson's place to get the letters back, but you didn't find them because they were never there. It wasn't Merson who stole them."

"I tell you it was!" retorted Broderick angrily. "I found a handkerchief with his initials on it."

"Exactly," said Henderson inscrutably. "You found a handkerchief, just as we expected."

Broderick caught his breath.

"You mean that handkerchief was planted? By God! What is this? A trap of some sort?"

He retreated to the centre of the room and backed against the overturned table.

"That story about Merson .. the accident. . . a fake?"

"Could be," said Henderson.

He saw Broderick flash a swift glance at the consulting room door, and guessed that he was assessing his chances of escape. Before he could make a move, however, the door opened and Inspector Ford came in. Ford looked worried. Disloyalty in a police officer seemed to him one of the cardinal sins.

"This looks like the end of the line, Broderick," he said quietly.

Broderick did not reply, but his left hand which had been tucked inside his coat suddenly moved to his mouth and they saw he had a white capsule between his first finger and thumb. Henderson sprang forward to grab Broderick's arm, but he was too late. Broderick staggered back on to the settee.

"Get Dr. Sheldon quickly," said Henderson.

Ford ran to the french windows and fumbled with the catch. The moment he was outside, Broderick suddenly sprang to life again, thrust Henderson aside and rushed for the consulting room door. When Henderson grabbed at him, Broderick brought his knee up sharply and the schoolmaster fell back, temporarily winded.

When he looked up he saw Broderick slam the consulting room door behind him, and there was a sound of the key turning in the lock. With a considerable effort he moved over and tried the door, then as he turned he saw Ford appear for a moment at the french windows, then vanish again. A few seconds later, there was a crash of glass inside the consulting room, then the sound of a scuffle. After that, a silence that seemed to last for minutes.

At length, Ford returned through the french windows.

"It's all right," he said, smiling, "the chaps outside got him as he came through the window." He looked across at Henderson, who was still trying to regain his breath.

"You all right?"

Henderson nodded and went over to the door leading to the hall, which he unlocked. As soon as she came in with Doctor Sheldon, Katherine noticed at once that he was suffering some pain, and was anxious to know what had happened. He assured her that he would be all right in a minute or two.

As Ford helped them to set the room to rights he said: "Thank you for your co-operation, Doctor. You, too, Miss Walters. This is just about the trickiest job I've come across."

"Don't ever ask me to do anything like that again!" declared Katherine fervently.

"Don't worry, miss, we won't." He hesitated, and turned to Doctor Sheldon. "I think you'd better take a look at the consulting room, sir. He's made rather a mess of the window—of course, we'll stand the cost of all that."

"Cheap at the price," grinned Henderson, as Sheldon departed to survey the damage. Katherine, who was still regarding Henderson with some concern, went and fetched him a drink. Ford refused one and said he would have to get back to the police station.

"I'd like you both to come down and sign a statement," he said. "Can I give you a lift now?"

Henderson looked at Katherine for a moment, then said: "I think we'd rather walk if you don't mind, Inspector. We'll be there in about twenty minutes."

"Suits me," nodded Ford. "In fact, it gives me a chance to clear up one or two things."

After the Inspector had gone, Henderson said: "I really think you should have a drink after that ordeal. You must be feeling pretty shaky."

"I'm tougher than you think," said Katherine.

"Were you frightened?" he asked, sipping his whisky.

"To be honest, I was terrified. Especially when he tore down the curtain and saw you standing there. I thought he would kill you."

"At that particular moment, I could feel nothing but relief that you were safely outside the room."

They looked at each other and smiled.

He finished his whisky and Katherine went out to tell her uncle that they were going to the police station.

Ten minutes later, they paused for a few moments on Medlow's ancient bridge to look at the lights reflected in the water.

"There's the houseboat where I first saw you that day . . ." she said presently, pointing to the shadowy out-fine of the boat that was in darkness. His hand closed over hers on the worn stone parapet.

"What are you thinking about?" she asked.

"Funnily enough . . . about Rocello's family motto."

'Family motto?"

"Yes, it's a very practical one. *Suaviter in modo . . .*"

Gentle in the manner," she said quietly, her hand tightening beneath his.

"But vigorous in the deed," concluded Henderson, and drew her face gently but firmly towards his own.

Printed in Great Britain
by Amazon

18827264R00103